No one writes romantic fiction like Barbara Cartland.

Miss Cartland was originally inspired by the best of the romantic novelists she read as a girl—Elinor Glyn, Ethel Dell, Ian Hay and E. M. Hull. Convinced that her own wide audience would also delight in her favorite authors, Barbara Cartland has taken their classic tales of romance and specially adapted them for today's readers.

Bantam is proud to publish these novels—personally selected and edited by Miss Cartland—under the imprint

BARBARA CARTLAND'S LIBRARY OF LOVE

Bantam Books by Barbara Cartland
Ask your bookseller for the books you have missed

1 THE DARING DECEPTION
2 NO DARKNESS FOR LOVE
3 THE LITTLE ADVENTURE
4 LESSONS IN LOVE
5 JOURNEY TO PARADISE
6 THE BORED BRIDEGROOM
7 THE PENNILESS PEER
8 THE DANGEROUS DANDY
9 THE RUTHLESS RAKE
10 THE WICKED MARQUIS
11 THE CASTLE OF FEAR
12 THE GLITTERING LIGHTS
13 A SWORD TO THE HEART
14 THE KARMA OF LOVE
15 THE MAGNIFICENT MARRIAGE
16 BEWITCHED
17 THE IMPETUOUS DUCHESS
18 THE FRIGHTENED BRIDE
19 THE SHADOW OF SIN
20 THE FLAME IS LOVE
21 THE TEARS OF LOVE
22 A VERY NAUGHTY ANGEL
23 CALL OF THE HEART
24 THE DEVIL IN LOVE
25 AS EAGLES FLY
26 LOVE IS INNOCENT
27 SAY YES, SAMANTHA
28 THE CRUEL COUNT
29 THE MASK OF LOVE
30 FIRE ON THE SNOW
31 AN ARROW OF LOVE
32 A GAMBLE WITH HEARTS
33 A KISS FOR THE KING
34 A FRAME OF DREAMS
35 THE FRAGRANT FLOWER
36 THE ELUSIVE EARL
37 MOON OVER EDEN
38 THE GOLDEN ILLUSION
39 THE HUSBAND HUNTERS
40 NO TIME FOR LOVE
41 PASSIONS IN THE SAND
42 THE SLAVES OF LOVE
43 AN ANGEL IN HELL
44 THE WILD CRY OF LOVE
45 THE BLUE-EYED WITCH
46 THE INCREDIBLE HONEYMOON
47 A DREAM FROM THE NIGHT
48 CONQUERED BY LOVE
49 NEVER LAUGH AT LOVE
50 THE SECRET OF THE GLEN
51 THE PROUD PRINCESS
52 HUNGRY FOR LOVE
53 THE HEART TRIUMPHANT
54 THE DREAM AND THE GLORY
55 THE TAMING OF LADY LORINDA
56 THE DISGRACEFUL DUKE
57 VOTE FOR LOVE

Barbara Cartland's Library of Love

1 THE SHEIK
2 HIS HOUR
3 THE KNAVE OF DIAMONDS
4 A SAFETY MATCH

Barbara
Cartland's
Library of Love

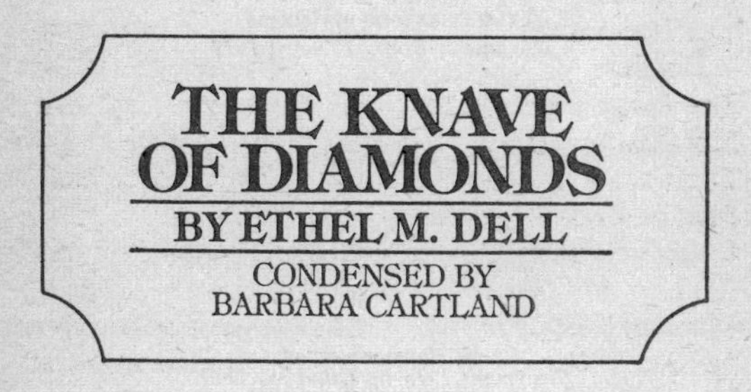
THE KNAVE
OF DIAMONDS
BY ETHEL M. DELL
CONDENSED BY
BARBARA CARTLAND

BANTAM BOOKS
TORONTO
NEW YORK
LONDON

THE KNAVE OF DIAMONDS

A Bantam Book / April 1977

ISBN 0-553-10527-2

Published simultaneously in the United States and Canada

Bantam Books are published by Bantam Books, Inc. Its trademark, consisting of the words "Bantam Books" and the portrayal of a bantam, is registered in the United States Patent Office and in other countries. Marca Registrada, Bantam Books, Inc., 666 Fifth Avenue, New York, New York 10019.

PRINTED IN THE UNITED STATES OF AMERICA

Preface
by
Barbara Cartland

Ethel M. Dell was the first romantic novelist I read and I remember being thrilled with her books which I borrowed for two pence from the Lending Library.

Her strong, passionate, often brutal heroes excited me, and her very feminine and elusive heroines were everything I was brought up to think a woman should be.

Her plots are always dramatic, always exciting and in *The Knave of Diamonds* one waits breathlessly for Nap to conquer and be conquered.

I believe it will bring you the pleasure and delight it has brought me for over sixty years.

Barbara Cartland

Chapter One

There came a sudden blare of music from the ball-room, and the woman who stood alone at an open window on the first floor shivered a little.

The room behind her was brilliantly lighted but empty. Some tables had been set for cards, but the cards were untouched. No one had penetrated to this refuge of the bored, no one save this tall and stately woman robed in shimmering, iridescent green, who stood with her face to the night.

Suddenly a man appeared with fierce dusky eyes. He looked the motionless figure up and down, then entered the room.

He was slight and clean-shaven, with high cheekbones that made a long jaw seem the leaner by contrast. His sleek black hair was parted in the middle above his swarthy face, giving an unmistakably foreign touch to his appearance. His tread was light and wary as a cat's.

He took up a pack of cards. He was counting them into heaps with lightning rapidity, turning up one here and there, and he did not raise his eyes as he spoke.

"You will have to tell me how old you are."

She wheeled round. The electric light flared upon her pale, proud face. She stood in dead silence, looking at him.

"You mustn't mind," he said persuasively. "I swear I'll never tell!"

Very quietly she turned and closed the window; then with a certain stateliness she advanced to the table at which he sat, and stopped before it.

"I think you are making a mistake," she said in a voice that had a hint of girlish sweetness about it despite its formality.

He looked up and the next instant was on his feet.

"Gad! I'm tremendously sorry! What must you take me for? I took you for Mrs. Damer. I beg you to forgive me."

She smiled a little, and some of the severity went out of her face.

"It is of no consequence. I saw it was a mistake."

"An idiotic mistake!" he declared with emphasis. "And you are not a bit like Mrs. Damer either. Are you waiting for someone? Would you like me to leave?"

"Certainly not. I am going myself."

"Oh, but don't!" he begged her very seriously. "I shall take it horribly to heart if you do. And really, I don't deserve such a snub as that."

Again she faintly smiled.

"I am not feeling malicious, but you are expecting your partner. And I . . ."

"No, I am not," he asserted. "My partner has deserted me for another fellow. I came in here merely because I was wandering about, seeking distraction. Please don't go—unless I bore you—in which case you have only to dismiss me."

She turned her eyes upon the cards before him.

"What are you doing with them? Is it a game?"

"Won't you sit down?" he said. "I will tell you."

She seated herself facing him.

He considered the cards for a little.

"It is a magician's game," he said. "Let me read your fortune."

She hesitated.

"You are not afraid?"

She met his look, a certain wistfulness in her grey eyes.

"Oh no, not afraid, only sceptical."

"Only sceptical!" he echoed. "That is a world-wide complaint. But anyone with imagination can always pretend. You are not good at pretending?"

"Not particularly."

There followed a few moments of silence; then in his careless drawl he said:

"Do you mind telling me your first name? It is essential to the game, of course, or I shouldn't presume to ask."

"My name is Anne."

The noise below had lessened considerably, and the tension had gone out of her bearing. She possessed that indescribable charm which attracts almost in spite of itself.

There was about her every movement a queenly grace that made her remarkable, and yet her face in repose had a look of unutterable weariness.

"How old are you, please?"

"Twenty-five."

He glanced up at her.

"Yes, twenty-five," she repeated.

"Do you like diamonds?"

She smiled at the question.

"Yes, I like them. I haven't a passion for them."

"No," he said, without raising his eyes. "You haven't a passion for anything at present. You will have soon."

"I think it very unlikely."

"Of course you do. Your eyes have not been opened yet. I see an exciting time before you. You are going to have an illness first. That comes in the near future."

"I have never been ill in my life."

"No? It will be an experience for you then, not a very painful one, I hope. Are you getting nervous?"

"Not in the least."

"Ah! That's as well, because here comes the King of Diamonds. He has taken a decided fancy to you, and if you have any heart at all, which I can't discover, you ought to end by being the Queen."

He paused.

"No, here comes the Knave—confound his impudence!—and by Jove, followed by the missing heart. I am glad you have got one anyway, even if the King is not in it. It looks as if you will have some trouble with that Knave, so beware of him."

He glanced up at her for a moment.

"Beware of him!" he repeated deliberately. "He is a dangerous scamp. The King is the man for you."

She received his caution with that faint smile of hers that softened her face but never seemed to reach her eyes.

He continued his contemplation of the cards for some seconds.

"I see an exciting future before you," he said finally. "I hope you will look out for me when you come into your own. I shall value Your Majesty's favour immensely."

"I will give you a place at Court as the Queen's jester."

He glanced up again sharply, met her smile, and bowed with much ceremony.

"Your Majesty's most humble servant! I enter upon my functions from this day forward. You will see my cap and bells in the forefront of the throng when you ride to your coronation."

"You are sure there will be a coronation?" she asked.

"It is quite evident," he replied with conviction.

"Even though I chance to be married already?"

He raised his brows.

"That rather complicates matters, doesn't it? Still it seems pretty certain. If it weren't for that hobgoblin of a Knave I should say it was quite so. He comes between the King and the heart, you see. I shouldn't be too intimate with him if I were you."

"I shall certainly keep him at a respectful distance. Now I must go."

Before she could answer they heard two people enter the door at the end of the card-room. It was separated by a screen and with a gesture he evoked silence and she obeyed.

"This is quite comfortable," said a woman's voice. "I am beginning to think the Hunt Ball is rather a farce, for it is impossible to dance."

"People don't know how to dance nowadays," grumbled Major Shirley in response. "I can't stand

these American antics. That young Nap Errol fa
sickens me."

"Oh, but he is a splendid dancer," protested his partner tolerantly.

"Of course you say so," growled the Major. "All women like that sort of whippersnapper. I call him a downright cad and I'm inclined to think him a blackguard as well. He wouldn't be tolerated if it weren't for his dollars, and they all belong to his brother, I'm told."

"He is a charming man. Such a pity he is a cripple!"

"He would probably be as insufferable as Nap if he weren't," rejoined the Major gloomily. "I wonder where he is."

"I expect he is stowed away in some corner well out of the way with his latest conquest. He won't turn up again this evening. He never does when once he goes to earth—the wily young fox.

"Who is his latest conquest, I wonder?" mused the woman. "I thought it was Mrs. Damer. But I have just seen her dancing with young Waring."

"Mrs. Damer! Why, that was the day before yesterday!" The Major laughed unpleasantly. " 'Anyone for a change, but no one for long' is Nap's motto.

"I wonder where my wife is. I'm tired of this show," the Major said testily. "They ought to build a Town Hall in this place, and do the thing properly."

"Now that there is a millionaire in the neighbourhood, it really might materialise. The Carfaxes would help, I am sure. Sir Giles is very open-handed."

"Drunken beast!" commented the Major. "A pretty spectacle he has been making of himself to-night. He is sitting in a corner of the refreshment-room absolutely incapable. He reached the noisy stage early in the evening. I am not sure that he even came sober."

"Isn't it too pitiful for words? That poor young wife of his! I can't think how she endures it; it must be positive martyrdom."

"Lady Carfax is a fool!" said the Major crossly. "I can't stand these martyrs. If she leads a dog's life it's her own fault. She's a fool to put up with it."

"Perhaps she can't help herself," pleaded the woman.

"Stuff and nonsense! No woman need be the slave of a drunken sot like that. She was his bailiff's daughter, you know, and people of that class don't generally suffer from an exaggerated sense of duty. She probably sticks to the man because she wants to keep in with the County."

"I must say I like Lady Carfax," broke in the woman with decision. "Whatever her origin, that queenliness of hers is not assumed. I believe her to be intensely reserved, and, perhaps for that very reason, I have a genuine admiration for her."

"My dear Mrs. Randal, you'd find points to admire in a wax candle," grunted the Major. "She always makes me think of one; pale and pure and saintly, I can't stand the type. Let's go downstairs and find Violet."

"Oh, not saintly, I think," protested Mrs. Randal charitably. "Saintly people are so uninteresting."

The Major laughed. He was already on his feet.

The voices fell away into the distance, and the woman on the other side of the screen rose to her feet.

Her companion's eyes were on her face as he said:

"Our gallant Major Shirley seems somewhat disgruntled tonight. Do you know him?"

"Yes, I know him."

"So do I." The man's tone was one of sheer amusement. "I had the pleasure of meeting him at the Rifle Club the other day. Someone introduced us. For some reason he wasn't pleased. Do you really want to go downstairs though? It is much nicer here."

"Yes," she said, and though still quiet her voice was not altogether even. "I want to go, please."

"May I tell you something first?" he asked. "It's not of paramount importance. But I think you may as well know, I am that wicked, wanton, wily fox, that whippersnapper, that unmitigated bounder . . . Nap Errol!"

He made the announcement with supreme complacence. It was evident that he felt not the faintest anxiety as to how she would receive it. She heard him with no sign of astonishment.

"I knew it," she said quietly. "I have known you by sight for some time."

"And you were not afraid to speak to such a dangerous scoundrel?" he said.

"You don't strike me as being very formidable," she answered. "Moreover, if you remember, it was you who spoke first."

"To be sure," he said. "It was all of a piece with my habitual confounded audacity. Shall I tell you something more? I wonder whether I dare."

"Wait!" she said imperatively. "It is my turn to tell you something, though it is more than possible that you know it already. Mr. Errol, I am . . . Lady Carfax!"

He bowed low.

"I did know," he said, in a tone from which all hint of banter had departed. "But I thank you none the less for telling me. I did not take you for Mrs. Damer in the card-room a little while ago. I took you for no one but yourself.

"I had been wanting to make your acquaintance all the evening. So I took the first opportunity that occurred, trusting to the end to justify the means."

"But why have you told me?" she said.

"Because I think you are a woman who appreciates the truth."

"I am," she said. "But I do not often hear it as I have heard it tonight."

He put out his hand to her impulsively.

"Lady Carfax, let me go and kick that old scandalmonger into the middle of next week!"

Involuntarily she gave him her hand.

"No, you mustn't," she said, laughing faintly.

"The fault was ours. You know the ancient adage about listeners. We deserved it all."

"Don't talk about deserves!" he exclaimed, with unexpected vehemence. "He doesn't deserve to have a whole bone left in his body. Neither do I for allowing him to go on talking."

She freed her hand gently.

"You could not have done otherwise. Believe me, I am not altogether sorry that you were with me when it happened. It is just as well that you should know the truth, and I could not have told it to you myself. Come, shall we go down?"

"Wait a minute!" he said. "Let me know how I stand with you first. Are you going to cut me next time we meet?"

"I shall not cut you," she said.

"You are going to acknowledge me then with the coldest of nods, which is even more damnable," he returned, with gloomy conviction.

She hesitated for an instant.

"Mr. Errol," she said gently, "will you believe me when I say that however I treat you in the future, you have helped me much more than you realize by your trifling tonight. I am not sure that you meant to do so. But I am grateful to you all the same."

"Then we are friends?" said Nap quickly.

"Yes, we are friends; but it is very unlikely that we shall meet again. I cannot invite you to call."

"And you won't call on my mother?" he asked.

"I am afraid not."

He was silent a moment.

"So be it!" he said. "But I fancy we shall meet again. *Au revoir,* Lady Carfax!"

"Good-bye, Sir Jester!" she replied.

He took her fingers and touched them with his lips.

"Farewell to Your Most Gracious Majesty!" he responded.

* * *

The Hunt Ball was over, and Mrs. Damer, wife of the M.F.H., was standing on the steps of the Carfax Arms, bidding the last member of the Hunt farewell."

Nap Errol was assisting her. He often did assist Mrs. Damer with that careless, half-insolent gallantry of his that no woman ever dreamed of resenting.

"Nap, I wish you would find my husband. I've said good-night to everybody, and I want to go home to bed."

"Lady Carfax hasn't gone yet," he observed. "I saw her standing in the doorway of the ladies' cloak-room just now."

"Lady Carfax! I thought they went long ago. Is their carriage waiting then?"

"Yes."

Mrs. Damer retired to the ladies' cloak-room. At her entrance Anne Carfax, clad in a white wrap, turned from the dying fire.

"My dear Lady Carfax!" exclaimed Mrs. Damer. "I quite thought you left ages ago. What is it? Is anything the matter?"

The pale lips smiled.

"No, nothing, thank you. I am only waiting for my husband."

"Then we are in the same plight. I am waiting for mine," Mrs. Damer replied.

"Sir Giles will not be long, I think."

"I will send Nap Errol to find him," said Mrs. Damer.

"Oh, no, thank you. That is quite unnecessary. Please do not trouble about me. A few minutes more or less make little difference."

The words came with the patience of deadly weariness.

"My dear Lady Carfax, you have the patience of a saint," Mrs. Damer explained, and bustled back into the hall.

"Are you there, Nap? Do see if you can find Sir Giles. Poor Lady Carfax is half-dead with cold and fit to drop with fatigue. Go and tell him so."

"Please do nothing of the sort," said Lady Carfax behind her. "No doubt he will come when he is ready."

Nap Errol looked from one to the other with swift comprehension in his glance.

"Let me put you into your carriage first, Mrs. Damer," he said. "Your husband is busy for the moment, some trifling matter. He begs you will not wait for him. I will drive him back in my motor. I have to pass your way, you know."

The Damer carriage moved down the street, and Nap Errol was once more beside Lady Carfax.

"Let me take you home in my motor," he begged. "No one will know."

She looked at him, her lips quivering a little.

"Thank you very much," she replied. "But I think not."

"No one will ever know," he reiterated. "I will just set you down at your own door and go away. Come, Lady Carfax!"

His dark eyes gazed straight into her own, determined, dominating. The high cheekbones and long, lean jaw looked as if fashioned in iron.

"Come!" he said again.

She made a slight movement as if to yield, and then drew back again.

"Really, I had better wait and go with my husband."

"You had better not!" he said with emphasis. "I have just seen him. I won't tell you what he is like. You probably know. But if you are a wise woman you will leave him for Damer to look after, and come with me."

That decided her. She threw the hood of her cloak over her head and turned to the door.

Errol paused to pull on an overcoat and then followed her onto the steps. A large covered motor had just glided up. He handed her into it, and he stepped in beside her after a word with the chauffeur, and shut the door.

Anne Carfax sank back in her corner and sat

motionless. The glare of the little electric lamp upon her face showed it white and tired. Her eyes were closed.

The man beside her sat bolt upright, his eyes fixed unblinkingly upon the window in front, his jaw set grimly. He held the gloves he had worn all the evening between his hands, and his fingers worked on them, rending the soft kid to ribbons.

They left the desolate street behind and came into total darkness.

Suddenly, but very quietly, Anne spoke.

"This is very kind of you, Mr. Errol."

He turned towards her. She had opened her eyes to address him, but the lids drooped heavily.

"The kindness is on your side, Lady Carfax," he said deliberately. "If you manage to inspire it in others, the virtue is still your own."

She smiled and closed her eyes again. It was evident that she did not desire to talk. He looked away from her, glanced at his torn gloves, and tossed them impatiently from him.

For ten minutes neither spoke. The car ran smoothly on through the night like a chariot of the gods. There was no sound of wheels. They seemed to be borne on wings.

For ten minutes the man sat staring stonily before him, rigid as a statue, while the woman sat passive by his side.

But at the end of that ten minutes the speed began to slacken. They came softly to earth and stopped.

Errol opened the door and alighted.

"Have you a key?" he asked, as he gave her his hand.

She stood above him, looking downwards half-dreamily as one emerging from a deep slumber.

"Do you know," she said, beginning to smile, "I thought that you were the Knave of Diamonds?"

"You've been asleep."

She gave a slight shudder as the night air brought her back, and in a moment, like the soft dropping of a veil, her reserve descended upon her.

"I am afraid I have," she said. "Please excuse me. Are we already at the Manor? Yes, I have the key."

She took his hand and stepped down beside him.

"Good-night, Mr. Errol, and thank you very much."

He did not offer to accompany her to the door. A light was burning within, and he merely waited till he heard the key turn in the lock.

Then he stepped back into the motor and slammed it shut, without any response to her last words.

Anne Carfax was left wondering if her dream had been a cause of offence.

* * *

"Oh, bother! It's cake morning." Dot Waring turned from the Rectory breakfast-table. "And I do so want to hear all about the Ball. You might have come down earlier, Ralph."

"My dear sister," said the Rector's son, "consider yourself lucky that I have come down at all after dancing half the night with Mrs. Damer, who is no light weight."

"You didn't, Ralph! I am quite sure you didn't! I'm not going to believe anything so absurd."

"All right. I didn't," said Ralph complacently.

"Was Bertie there?" she asked.

"Bertie who?"

"Bertie Errol, of course. Who else?"

"There are plenty of Berties in the world," remarked Ralph. "No, Bertram Errol was not present. But Napoleon Errol was. It was he who shunted Mrs. Damer onto me. Give Napoleon Errol a wide berth in future. He has the craft of a conjurer and the subtlety of a serpent. I believe he is a Red Indian."

"Oh, Ralph, he isn't! He is as white as you are."

"He isn't white at all," Ralph declared, "outside or in. Outside he is the colour of a mangold-wurzel, and inside he is as black as ink. You will never get that cake made if you don't go."

"Oh, bother!" Dot swung open the door, and then exclaimed in a very different tone, "Why, Bertie, so here you are! We were just talking of you."

A straight well-made youth, with a sunburnt face, laughing good-temperedly, was advancing through the hall.

"Hullo!" he said. "What were you saying, I wonder?"

"I am going to bake cakes," answered Dot.

"I'll come and bake cakes too," said Bertie promptly.

"Why didn't you go to the Hunt Ball last night?" Dot asked.

"My brother wasn't so well yesterday. I was reading to him half the night."

"You are very good to your brother."

"Good to him! Great Scot! Why, he's miles too good for any of us. Don't ever class him with Nap or me! We're just ordinary sinners. But he—he's a king."

"You are awfully fond of him, aren't you?" said Dot sympathetically.

"Fond of Lucas! I'd die for him!" the boy declared with feeling. "He's father and brother and friend to me. There isn't anything I wouldn't do for him. Did you ever hear how he came to be a cripple?"

"Never," said Dot.

"He was knocked down by an electric car," Bertie said, "trying to save his best girl's dog from being run over. He did save it, but he was frightfully hurt, paralyzed for months. It's years ago now. But I shall never forget it. I thought he was done for."

"And the girl?" asked Dot rather breathlessly.

"She married an English nobleman," he answered.

"I should like to meet your brother," Dot remarked. "I've never spoken to a real flesh-and-blood hero in my life."

"Nothing easier," said Bertie promptly. "Come

over and have tea. Come this afternoon, you and Ralph."

But Dot hesitated, in evident doubt.

"I don't know what Dad would say."

"My mother would be delighted. Come early and I'll show you the hunters. Nap has just bought a beauty. She's a blood mare, black as ink."

"Like Nap," said Dot absently; then in haste, "No, I didn't mean that."

Bertie was looking at her shrewdly. "What do you know about Nap?"

She coloured deeply. "Nothing, nothing whatever. I only know him by sight."

"And you don't like him?"

"I . . . I think he looks rather wicked," she stammered. "And my father doesn't want me to meet him, unless I am obliged."

She uttered the last words in evident distress. Bertie's face had grown quite serious, even stern.

"I guess your father knows what he's about," he said at length, "but it beats me to understand why he has me here to study. I guess I'd better shunt."

"Oh, please don't!" she said quickly. "It isn't you at all. It's only Nap."

"Damn Nap!" said Bertie, with some fervour. "Well, I'm not a blackguard anyway, and I never shall be if you keep on being kind to me. Is that understood?"

* * *

It was a week after the Hunt Ball that Anne Carfax, sitting alone at tea in her drawing-room, was surprised at the announcement of old Dimsdale the butler.

"Mr. Nap Errol to see Your Ladyship!"

She rose to meet him, her surprise in her face, and he, entering with that light, half-stealthy tread of his, responded to it before his hand touched hers.

"I know my presence is unexpected, and my welcome precarious, but as none of my friends have been able to give me any news of you, I determined to chance my reception and come myself to inquire for your welfare."

"You are very good," said Anne, but she spoke with a certain stateliness, and there was no pleasure in her eyes.

"I am beginning to think I must be," he said, "since you say so. I know you to be strictly truthful."

Anne made no response. She did not even smile.

"I am in luck to find you alone," proceeded Nap, surveying her with cold, dark eyes that were nothing daunted by her lack of cordiality.

"My husband will be in soon," she answered quietly.

"I shall be delighted to make his acquaintance," said Nap imperturbably. "Has he been hunting?"

"Yes." Anne's tone was distant.

"You ought to hunt," he said. "Why don't you?"

"I do . . . occasionally."

"What's the good of that? You ought to regularly. There's nothing like it." He smiled upon her disarmingly. "Are you wondering if I take one lump or two? I take neither, and no milk, please."

Against her will she faintly smiled.

"I thought that was it," said Nap. "Why didn't you ask me? Are these scones in the fender? May I offer you one?"

He dropped upon his knees to pick up the dish, and in that attitude humbly proffered it to her.

She found it impossible to remain ungracious. She could only seat herself at the tea-table and abandon the attempt.

"Sit down and help yourself," she said.

He pulled a large hassock to him and sat facing her.

"Now we can be sociable," he said. "Really, you know, you ought to hunt more often. I have never seen you in the field once. What on earth do you do with yourself?"

"Many things," said Anne.

"What things?" he persisted.

"I help my husband to the best of my ability with the estate and try to keep an eye on the poorest tenants. And then I practice the piano a good deal. I haven't time for much besides."

"I say, do you play?" said Nap, keenly interested. "I do myself, a little, not the piano—the violin. Lucas likes it, or I suppose I should have given it up long ago."

Anne's face reflected his interest.

"Tell me more about it," she said. "What sort of music do you care for?"

"Oh, anything, from Christmas carols to sonatas. I never play to please myself, and Lucas has very varied tastes."

"He is your elder brother?" questioned Anne.

"Yes, and one of the best. He is hopelessly crippled, poor chap, and suffers infernally. I often wonder why he puts up with it. I should have shot myself long ago, had I been in his place."

"Perhaps he is a good man," Anne said.

He shot her a keen glance.

"What do you mean by a good man?"

"I mean a man who does his duty without shirking."

"Is that your ideal?" he said. "There are plenty of men that do that, and yet their lives are anything but blameless."

"Quite possibly," she agreed. "But if a man does his duty, he has not lived in vain. It can be no man's duty to destroy himself."

"And how would you define 'duty'?" said Nap.

She let her eyes meet his for a moment.

"I can only define it for myself."

"Will you do so for me?" he asked.

A faint colour rose to her face. There was a deep sadness about her lips as she made reply.

"I have not been given much to do. I have to content myself with 'the work that's nearest.' "

Nap was watching her closely.

"And if I did the same," he questioned in a drawl that was unmistakably supercilious, "should I be a good man?"

"I don't know what your capabilities are," she said.

"I have vast capabilities for evil," he told her, with a cynical twist of his thin-lipped mouth.

She met his look again.

"I am sorry."

"Are you really? But why? Doesn't the devil attract you? Honestly now! I have told you frankly, but I am not what you would call a good man. But, the truth, mind!—would you like me any better if I were?"

She smiled a little. There was undoubted fascination in the upturned face with its fiery eyes and savage jaw. Perhaps the lips were cruel, but they were very sensitive.

She did not answer him immediately, and during the pause his eyes never flinched from hers. They were alive, glowing with insistence.

"Yes," she said at length. "Quite honestly, I do prefer good men."

"That wasn't exactly what I asked," said Nap.

"I think you are capable of drawing your own conclusions," she answered gently.

His look fell away from her.

The silence became lengthy. She was conscious of something in the atmosphere that made her vaguely uneasy.

This was a man of many subtleties, she knew it instinctively, a man of tigerish temperament, harmless as a kitten in sunshine, merciless as a fiend in storm. Yes, he was certainly like a tiger, forcible even in repose.

She had never before encountered so dominant a personality. It affected her strangely, half-attractive, half-repelling, arousing in her a sense of antagonism that yet was not aversion.

"I wish you would say all that out loud," said Nap. "You have such interesting thoughts, it is really selfish of you not to express them."

"Surely not," she said, "if you know what they are."

He gave her an odd look as he lifted his teacup.

"The Queen's jester is a privileged person," he said. "When the door of her pleasance is closed to him he climbs up and looks over the wall."

An unsteady hand began to fumble at the door, and Anne glanced up with a start. The blood rose to her face.

"I think it is my husband," she said in a low voice.

Nap did not turn his head or answer. He sat motionless, still staring at her, till the door began to open. Then, with a sudden, lithe movement, he rose and kicked the hassock to one side.

A big man in riding-dress tramped heavily into the room, and stopped in the centre, peering before him under scowling brows.

He looked about fifty, to judge by his iron-grey hair and moustache, but he might have been less.

"This is Mr. Nap Errol, Giles. Mr. Errol . . . my husband."

"I have been waiting for the pleasure of meeting you," Nap drawled. "I dropped in on the chance, and Lady Carfax assured me you wouldn't be long."

Sir Giles scowled more heavily than before. He shot a malignant glance at his wife.

"Who in thunder made her so clever?" he growled. "And what did you want to see me for? Have I ever met you before?"

His voice was thick, the words somewhat difficult to distinguish.

Nap's smile was unmistakably sardonic.

"Many times," he said. "You nearly rode over me on the last occasion. Doubtless the episode has escaped your memory, but it made a more lasting impression upon mine."

Sir Giles glared offensively.

"I remember," he said. "Your animal came down with you. You pushed in front of me. But it was your own fault. You Americans never observe the rules of sport. I'm always glad to see you come a-cropper."

"I am sure of it," said Nap politely. "It must gratify you immensely."

Sir Giles uttered a brief, snarling laugh, and advanced abruptly to the hearth.

Nap was quite ready with his answer.

"I am really here on my brother's behalf. There is a scheme afoot, as no doubt you know, for the building of a Town Hall. My brother considers that the Lord of the Manor"—he bowed with thinly veiled irony—"should have first say in the matter. But I am at liberty to assure you that should you be in favour of the scheme he is ready to offer you his hearty support."

Sir Giles heard him out with lowering brows.

"I am not in favour of the scheme," he said shortly.

Nap slightly raised his brows.

"No? I understood otherwise."

The blood mounted to Sir Giles's forehead.

"Either you were misinformed or your intelligence is at fault," he said, with that in his voice that was so nearly an open insult that even Nap looked for a second dangerous.

Then quietly, without raising her eyes, Anne intervened.

"I think you ought to explain to Mr. Errol, Giles, that you have only recently changed your mind."

Sir Giles rounded on her malignantly.

"What the devil has that to do with it, or with you, for that matter? Do you think I don't know my own mind? Do you think . . ."

"I know exactly what Lady Carfax thinks," cut in Nap, moving deliberately so that he stood directly between Sir Giles and the tea-table.

"And in the main, I agree with her, though my sentiments are a little stronger than hers. But with regard to this Town Hall suggestion, what's wrong with it? Couldn't you come over and talk it out with my brother? He isn't well enough just now to come to you."

The coolness of this speech took effect. Sir Giles glared for a few moments till the speaker's steady regard became too much for him. Then, with a lurching movement, he turned away.

"No, I won't visit your brother! Why the deuce should I? Do you think I belong to the rag, tag, and bobtail, that I'll mix with the very scum of society so long as there's money about? Do you think I'd lower myself to associate with fellows like you?"

"I guess you'd find it difficult," drawled Nap.

He still stood with his back to the tea-table. He was unquestionably master of the situation, without much apparent effort.

Sir Giles knew himself to be worsted, and in his wife's presence. He glanced at her through eyes narrowed to evil slits. Her very impassivity goaded him. It seemed in some fashion to express contempt. With violence he strode to the bell and peeled it vigorously.

On the instant Nap turned.

"So long, Lady Carfax!"

She looked up at him. Her lips said nothing, but for that instant her eyes entreated, and his eyes made swift response.

He was smiling with baffling good humour as he turned round to Sir Giles.

"Good-bye, sir! Delighted to have met you. I'll give your message to my brother. It'll amuse him."

He departed without a backward glance as the servant opened the door, elaborately deaf to Sir Giles's half-strangled reply that he might go to the devil and take his brother with him.

Sir Giles, livid, stammering with rage, strode up

and down and cursed the departed visitor in lurid language, cursed the errand that had brought him, and rated his wife for admitting him.

"I will not know these impertinent, opulent Americans!" was the burden of his maledictions. "As for that damned, insolent bounder, the man's a blackguard. And if I ever catch him alone in your company after this, I'll thrash him—do you hear?—I'll thrash him! So now you know what to expect."

It was at this point that Anne rose, passed quietly, with the bearing of a Queen, down the long room, and without a word closed the door very softly behind her.

Chapter Two

On one occasion, and one only, in the whole year were the gates of the Manor thrown open to all comers, when the fox-hounds met upon the Manor lawn.

Anne, clad in the conventional black riding-habit that only added grace to her severity of outline, moved among her husband's guests.

Little Dot Waring marked her progress with

looks of loving admiration. Lady Carfax's mount, a powerful grey with nervous ears and gleaming eyes, was being held close to them.

"Be ready to mount her when she comes this way, Ralph," Dot whispered.

But the honour of mounting Lady Carfax was not for Ralph. A man on a black mare, a slight man with high cheekbones and an insolent bearing, was threading his way towards them through the crowd.

Bertie, looking very handsome and stalwart, was already close to them. He leaned down from the saddle to shake hands as Nap rode towards them.

Bertie's expression altered as his glance fell upon his brother.

"Hold the mare a minute, will you?" Nap asked.

Bertie complied and he swung himself to the ground.

Lady Carfax was coming towards them and he went to meet her. Her grey eyes smiled a friendly welcome.

"I was just wondering if you were here."

"I am honoured indeed to be in your thoughts for a single instant."

"I hope I do not forget my friends so easily," she said. "Oh, here are some more of them! Excuse me for a moment."

She went straight to Dot, shook hands with her and Ralph.

Nap remained close behind her, and after a little she turned to include him in the group.

"Have you ever met this Mr. Errol, Dot? Mr. Errol—Miss Waring!"

"And you don't know Bertie Errol, do you, Lady Carfax?" Dot said eagerly. "Let me introduce him. He studies with Dad, you know."

Lady Carfax smiled and turned towards her mount. Ralph moved to assist her, but Nap pushed him aside.

"My job, I think," he drawled, with an expression on his face which made the youth draw back.

In a few minutes more the hunt was off. The sun shone through a mist. The weather was perfect for hunting, but looked as if it might end in rain.

Sir Giles rode with the master. He seemed in better spirits than usual. His customary scowl had lifted.

His wife was nearer the end of the field, with Nap Errol next to her. His brother was immediately behind them.

"Get on ahead, Bertie! I can't stand you riding at my heels," Nap said sharply.

Bertie rode ahead and Nap smiled.

"That young puppy is the best of the Errol bunch."

"He looks a nice boy," Anne said. "But there is a considerable difference between you?"

"Eight years," said Nap. "I am thirty, Lucas is five years older. Most people take me for the eldest of the lot."

"I wonder why," said Anne.

He shrugged his shoulders.

"It is not really surprising, is it? Lucas has been on the shelf for the past ten years, and I"—he glanced at her shrewdly—"have not!"

"Oh!" said Anne, and asked no more.

For the first time the definite question arose in her mind as to whether in admitting this man to her friendship she had made a mistake. She was forced to acknowledge that he had a disquieting effect upon her.

Yet as they drifted apart in the throng, she knew with unalterable conviction that the matter did not rest with her.

He had entered the gates of her lonely citadel on the night of the Hunt Ball, and she realized that it was too late now to try to bar him out.

* * *

They found a fox after some delay in a copse on the side of a hill, and the run that followed scattered even Anne's sedateness to the winds.

The grey went like the wind. He and the black mare that Nap Errol rode led the field, a distinction that Anne had never sought before.

When they killed in a chalky hollow, she dragged her animal round with a white, set face and forced him from the scene. Nap followed her after a little and found her fumbling at a gate into a wood.

"I've secured the brush for you," he began. Then, seeing her face. "What is it? You look sick."

"I feel sick," she said shakily.

He opened the gate for her and followed her through. They found themselves alone, separated from the rest of the hunt by a thick belt of trees.

"Do you mean to say you have never seen a kill before?" he said.

"Never at close quarters," murmured Anne, with a shudder.

He rode for a little in silence.

"I'm sorry you didn't like being in at the death," he said. "I thought you would be pleased."

"Pleased!" she said, and shuddered again.

"Personally," said Nap, "I enjoy a kill."

Anne's face expressed horror.

"Yes," he said recklessly, "I am like that. I hunt to kill. It is my nature."

A red gleam shone suddenly in his fiery eyes. He looked at her aggressively.

"What do you hunt for anyway?"

"I don't think I shall hunt any more," she replied.

"Oh, nonsense, Lady Carfax! That's being ultra-squeamish," he protested.

"I can't help it," she said. "I never realized before how cruel it is."

"Of course it's cruel," said Nap. "But then so is everything, so is life. We were created to prey on each other."

"No, no!" she said quickly, for his words hurt her inexplicably. "I take the higher view."

"I beg your pardon," said Nap, in the tone of one refusing a discussion.

She turned to him impulsively.

"Surely you do too!" she said, and there was even a note of pleading in her voice.

Nap's brows met suddenly. He turned his eyes away.

"I am nothing but an animal. There is nothing spiritual about me. I live for what I can get. If I have a soul at all, it is so rudimentary as to be unworthy of mention."

In the silence that followed he looked at her again, with grim comprehension.

"P'r'aps you don't care for animals," he suggested cynically. "To change the subject, do you know we are leaving the hunt behind?"

She reined in somewhat reluctantly.

"I suppose we had better go back."

"If Your Majesty decrees," said Nap.

He pulled the mare round and stood motionless, waiting for her to pass. He sat arrogantly at his ease. She could not fail to note that his horsemanship was magnificent. The mare stood royally as though she bore a King.

"Will you lead the way?" he asked.

And Anne passed him with a vague sense of uneasiness. It seemed to her as if he had imposed his will upon hers, and made her acknowledge his mastery.

Rejoining the hunt, she made a deliberate attempt to avoid him.

At the next draw the fox headed for the Baronmead Woods, and after him streamed the hunt. But it was not Anne's intention to be in at a second death that day.

The mist was thickening in the valley, and it had begun to drizzle. The watch on her wrist said two o'clock, and she determined to turn her face homewards.

She shivered as the chill damp crept about her. A feeling of loneliness that was almost physical possessed her. She half-wished that she had not forsaken the hunt after all.

Stay! Was she quite alone? Out of the clinging ever-thickening curtain there came the sound of hoofs and a man's voice.

Her heart gave a sudden sharp throb. She knew that voice. Why had he elected to come that way? she asked herself. He almost seemed to be dogging her steps.

Impulse urged her to strike in another direction before he reached her. She did not feel inclined for another tête-à-tête with Nap Errol.

She tapped the grey smartly with her switch, more smartly than she had intended, for he started and plunged. At the same instant there broke out immediately below them a hubbub of yelling and baying.

It rose up through the fog as from the mouth of an invisible pit. The grey horse reared bolt upright, pawed the air wildly, flung out his heels, and bolted down the hill, straight for the pandemonium of men and hounds.

For the first few seconds of that mad flight Anne was taken by surprise and was forced to give all her attention to keeping in the saddle.

The pace was terrific. The scampering hoofs

scarcely seemed to touch the ground. Like shadows they fled through the rising mist. She seemed to be plunging into an icy, bottomless abyss.

Then like a dagger, stabbing through every nerve, came fear, a horror unspeakable of the depth she could not see, into which she was being so furiously hurled. She was clinging to the saddle, but she made a desperate effort to drag the animal round.

It was quite fruitless. No woman's strength could have availed to check that headlong gallop. He swerved a little, a very little, in answer, that was all, and galloped madly on.

And then, all in a moment it came, a moment of culminating horror more awful than anything she had ever before experienced. The ground fell suddenly away from the racing feet.

A confusion of many lights danced before her eyes, a buzzing uproar filled her brain, she shot forward into space. . . .

* * *

Sir Giles was in a decidedly evil temper as he rode home from the hunt in the soaking rain that afternoon. Dusk had long descended when at length he turned in at his own gates.

Hearing a clatter of hoofs on the drive before him, he roused himself to hollo into the darkness, supposing that his wife was ahead of him. If it were she, she was later in returning than was her wont, but no answer came back to him, and he did not repeat his call.

After all, why should he hail her? He did not

want her company, heaven knew. That stately demeanour which once had attracted him now inspired a savage sense of resentment.

He heard the sound of a horse's feet some distance in front. They seemed to fall unevenly, as if the animal was lame. Could it be the grey? he asked himself. If so, why had Anne not answered his call? She must have heard him.

He ground his teeth. It was like her habitual impudence to ignore him thus. He gathered himself together and sent a furious bellow into the darkness.

Three minutes later he rode heavily into his own stableyard. A group of servants scattered dumbly before him as he appeared. He fancied that they looked at him strangely. He flung an oath at the groom who stepped forward to take his horse.

"What are you staring at? What's the matter?"

The man murmured something unintelligible.

Sir Giles dismounted and scowled round.

"You look like a crowd of death's heads," he growled. "Hullo! What's this?"

He had caught sight of something he had not seen before, something that sent him striding furiously forward. In the centre of the yard, standing on three legs, was the grey horse his wife had ridden.

Limp and draggled, plastered with mud and foam, with a great streaming gash on the shoulder; the grey's head was hanging down in utter exhaustion.

"What's this?" demanded Sir Giles again. "Where's Her Ladyship?"

"The animal's come home alone, Sir Giles," old Dimsdale the butler replied.

"What?"

The old man faced his master with respectful firmness.

"As I said, Sir Giles, the animal's come back alone."

"Only just come in, Sir," chimed in a groom. "Looks as if Her Ladyship has met with a haccident."

Sir Giles rounded upon him with violence. Then, having worked off the first heat of his fury, he turned again to Dimsdale.

"What the devil is to be done? I never saw her after the first kill."

"And where might that have been, Sir Giles?"

"Up Baronmead way. It was hours ago."

Dimsdale considered.

"Shall we send and make inquiries at Baronmead, Sir Giles?"

"No! I'm damned if I do! Was Her Ladyship riding with anyone in particular?" Dimsdale asked next.

"No, I don't think so. Say! I believe I saw that Errol bounder talking to her. But I won't have any traffic with them. I've said I won't and I won't."

"Seems to me the only thing to do, Sir Giles,"

Dimsdale insisted. "You can't leave Her Ladyship to die under a hedge, and not do anything to find her."

He looked straight into his master's bloodshot eyes as he spoke.

"It wouldn't be hardly right, Sir Giles," he pointed out gravely. "It's likely that young Mr. Errol will be able to give us a clue, and we can't leave any stone unturned. I'll send on my own responsibility if you like, Sir Giles. But send we must."

With a shrug Sir Giles turned away from him.

"Oh, go your own way, and be damned to you! Don't stand gaping there, you fools! Get to your work! Better send for the vet. Can't afford to have a valuable animal spoilt. Dimsdale, take some brandy and hot water up to my room before you do anything else. Do you hear?"

Some time later the door of his room opened softly, and old Dimsdale entered.

"We have news, Sir Giles."

Sir Giles neither looked at him nor spoke.

"A messenger has just come from Baronmead, Sir Giles," he said, speaking very distinctly. "Her Ladyship had a fall, and has been taken there. Mr. Errol begs that you will go back in the motor, as Her Ladyship's condition is considered serious."

He stopped. Sir Giles said nothing whatever.

"The messenger is waiting, Sir Giles."

Still no response of any sort.

Dimsdale waited a moment, then very respectfully he bent and touched his master's shoulder.

"Sir Giles!"

Sir Giles turned slowly at last, with immense effort it seemed.

"Bring some brandy and water," he said, "hot!"

"But the messenger, Sir Giles!"

"Tell him to go to the devil!" he thundered. "And when you've done that, bring me some brandy and water—hot!"

When Dimsdale returned he was sunk in the chair asleep.

* * *

"Hullo, Lucas! Can I come in?"

Nap Errol stood outside his brother's door, an impatient frown on his face.

"Come in, old chap," drawled back a kindly voice.

He entered with an abruptness that seemed to denote agitation.

In an easy chair by the fire the eldest Errol was reclining, while his valet, a huge man with the features of an American Indian half-breed and fiery red hair, put the finishing touches to his evening-dress.

Nap approached the fire with his usual noiseless tread despite the fact that he was still in riding-boots.

"Be quick, Hudson!" he said. "We don't want you."

Hudson rolled a nervous eye at him and became clumsily hasty.

"Take your time," his master said quietly. "Nap, my friend, hadn't you better dress?"

Nap stopped before the fire and pushed it with his foot.

"I am not going to dine," he said.

Lucas Errol said no more. He lay quite motionless. Hudson, the valet, tended him with the reverence of a slave.

Nap paced soundlessly to and fro, waiting with what patience he could muster.

"You can go now, Tawny," the elder Errol drawled at last. "I will ring when I want you. Now, Boney, what is it? How is Lady Carfax?"

Nap sat down with some reluctance. He looked as if he would have preferred to prowl.

"She is still unconscious, and likely to remain so. The doctor thinks very seriously of her."

"Her husband has been informed?"

"Her husband," said Nap from between his teeth, "has been informed, and he declines to come to her. That's the sort of brute he is."

Lucas Errol made no comment, and Nap continued:

"It is just as well perhaps. I hear he is never sober after a day's sport. And I believe she hates the sight of him, if the truth were told, and small wonder!"

There was unrestrained savagery in the last words. Lucas turned his head and looked at him thoughtfully.

"You know her rather well?" he said.

"Yes." Nap's eyes, glowing redly, met his with a gleam of defiance.

"You have known her for long?"

"I don't estimate friendships by time."

Lucas said no more, but he continued to look at his brother with unvarying steadiness till at length, as if goaded thereto, Nap spoke again.

"We are friends," he said, "no more, no less. You all think me a blackguard, I know. It's my specialty, isn't it? But in this case you are wrong. I repeat—we are friends."

He said it aggressively; his tone was almost a challenge, but the elder Errol did not appear to notice.

"I have never thought you a blackguard, Boney," he said quietly.

Nap's thin lips smiled cynically.

"You have never said it."

"I have never thought it. What does the doctor say about her?"

"He says very little. After the manner of his tribe, he is afraid to commit himself. I shall get someone down from town tomorrow. I'd go tonight, only . . ."

He broke off, hammering impotently with his clenched fist on the arm of his chair.

"I must be at hand tonight," he continued, after a moment. "The mater has promised to call me if there is any change. You see, Lady Carfax might feel kind of lonely waking up in a crowd of strangers, and mine is the only face she knows."

Nap sat with his face to the fire, and stared unblinkingly into the red depths.

Softly at length his brother's voice came through the silence.

"Why not dine while you are waiting? You will do no good to anyone by starving yourself."

"In heaven's name, don't talk to me of eating!" he said savagely. "You don't know what I've been through. I thought she was dead."

A sudden shudder shook him. He got up and vigorously poked the fire.

Lucas Errol endured the clatter for several seconds in silence.

"Since you are feeling so energetic, Boney," he said, "you might lend me a hand."

Nap laid down the poker instantly.

"I am sorry, old fellow. I forgot. Let me ring for Hudson."

"Can't you help me yourself?"

Nap hesitated a second; then stooped in silence to give the required assistance. Lucas Errol, with a set face, accepted it, but once on his feet he leaned upon the mantlepiece to wipe his forehead.

"I knew I should hurt you," Nap said uneasily.

"Never mind me!" Lucas replied. "It is your affairs that trouble me just now, not my own. And, Boney, if you don't have a meal soon, you'll be making a big fool of yourself and everyone will know it."

The very gentleness of his speech seemed to

make the words the more insistent. Nap raised no further protest.

"Go and have it right now," Lucas said quietly.

* * *

What had happened?

Anne had been horribly afraid. She seemed to be yet falling, falling through emptiness to annihilation. And as she fell she caught the sounds of other worlds, vague whisperings in the dark.

She was sinking, sinking fast into a depth unfathomable, where no worlds were. Then out of the chaos and awful darkness a hand reached out and grasped her own. A hand strong and vital that gripped and lifted her up, guided and sustained her.

The light dawned gradually in her eyes. She found herself gazing up into a face she knew, a lean brown face, alert and keen, that watched her steadfastly.

With an effort she clasped her nerveless fingers upon the sustaining hand.

"Hold me!" she whispered weakly. "I'm falling!"

"Don't be afraid!" he made answer with infinite gentleness. "I have you safe."

He moved slightly, took something into his free hand and held it to her lips. Submissively, in answer to an influence that seemed gently to compel, she drank.

Slowly the mist of dread cleared from her brain. She awoke to full consciousness, and found

Nap Errol bending over her, her hand fast clasped in his.

"What happened?" she asked him faintly. "Where am I?"

"You are at Baronmead," he said. "You were thrown, and we brought you here."

"Am I much hurt?" she asked.

"Nothing to worry about," Nap said, with quiet confidence. "You will soon be all right again. I will leave you to get a good sleep. If you are wanting anything, my mother will be here."

She looked at him doubtfully. Her hand still clung to his.

"Mr. Errol," she faltered, "my husband . . . does he know?"

"Yes, he knows." Very softly Nap made answer, as though he were soothing a child. "Don't trouble about it. Don't trouble about anything. Just lie still and rest."

But the anxiety in her eyes was growing.

"He isn't here?" she questioned.

"No."

"Then . . . then I think I ought to go to him. He will think it so strange. He will . . . he will . . ."

"Lady Carfax, listen!" Quietly but insistently he broke in upon her rising agitation. "Your husband knows all about you. He couldn't come tonight, but he is coming in the morning. Now won't you be content and try to sleep?"

"I can't sleep," she said with a shudder. "I am afraid of falling."

"No, you're not. See! I am holding your hands. You can't fall. Look at me! Keep looking at me and you will see how safe you are!"

His voice had sunk almost to a whisper. His eyes, dusky, compelling, yet strangely impersonal, held hers by some magic that was too utterly intangible to frighten her. With a sigh she yielded to the mastery she scarcely felt.

* * *

When Anne opened her eyes again it was many hours later, and she was lying in the broad sunshine, with the doctor, whom she knew, stooping over her.

"Ah, you are awake at last!" he said. "And I find a marvellous improvement. No, I shouldn't try to move at present. You have had a wonderful escape, my dear lady, a most wonderful escape.

"But for all that I shall keep you where you are for the next fortnight or so. A badly jarred spine is not a thing to play with."

"Is that all?" Anne asked.

"I don't say that it is all. In any case we will run no risks. Let me congratulate you upon having fallen into such good hands."

He glanced over Anne's head at someone on the other side of the bed, and Anne turned slightly to see the person thus indicated. And so she had her first sight of the woman who ruled Lucas Errol's house.

Large-boned, large-featured, and stout, her voice was as deep as a man's, and it went even deeper when she laughed.

"I'm Mrs. Errol, dear," she said. "And if there's anything you want . . . well, you've only got to mention it to me and it's as good as done."

"You are very good," Anne murmured.

"Not a bit," said Mrs. Errol cheerfully. "I'm real pleased to have you."

The next day Anne was possessed by a nervous dread that increased steadily as the hour wore on. At last she summoned her resolutions and compelled herself to speak.

"My husband has not come yet?" she asked.

"No, dear." Mrs. Errol smiled upon her with much kindness.

"Did he send no message?" she asked with knitted brows. "I thought . . . or did I dream it? . . . that your son said he was coming."

"To be sure he did," said Mrs. Errol. "You would like to speak to Nap about it, wouldn't you?"

"No, please!" she said, a slight flush on her face. "Don't call him in again! Really, it is of no consequence."

As the hours passed, the torture of suspense so worked upon her that she began to grow feverish. The afternoon was waning and still no word had come.

She tried to reassure herself again and again, but each failure added to her distress.

"You mustn't fret, child," said Mrs. Errol gently, when she brought her tea. "It's the worst thing possible."

Mrs. Errol said no more, but presently she

went quietly away, leaving her alone in the firelight, chafing but impotent.

She was soon back again, however, and saw behind her Nap, slim, upright, and noiseless, come to the bedside. He stooped a little and took Anne's quivering hand, holding it in both his own so that his fingers pressed upon her pulse.

"The mater thought you would like to speak to me," he said.

"Oh, Nap," she said, admitting him unconsciously in her extremity to an intimacy she would never have dreamed of according him in any less-urgent circumstance, "I am greatly troubled about my husband. You said he would come to me, but he hasn't come!"

"I know he hasn't," Nap said.

He spoke quietly, but she was aware of a certain grimness in his speech.

"I shouldn't worry if I were you. It won't help you any. Is there anyone else you would like to see?"

"I have no one else," she said, her voice quivering beyond her control. "How can I lie here and not worry?"

"Lord, bless the child!" said Mrs. Errol vigorously. "What is there to worry about, anyway?"

But Nap was silent. His fingers were still closed firmly upon her wrist.

"Mrs. Errol is very good. You mustn't think me ungrateful or unappreciative," Anne said earnestly. "But I cannot go on like this. I cannot!"

"I am afraid you have no choice," Nap said.

"Will you tell me exactly what has passed? Has he definitely refused to come to me? Because, if so . . ."

"If so . . ." said Nap gently.

She summoned her wavering self-control.

"If so . . . I must go back to him at once. I must, indeed. You will manage it for me, will you not? Perhaps you will take me in the motor."

"No," said Nap.

He spoke briefly, even sternly. He was bending down over her, and she caught the gleam of the firelight in his eyes and thought that they shone red.

"I would do a good deal for you, Lady Carfax," he said, "but I can't do that. You ask the impossible."

He paused a moment and she felt his grasp slowly tighten upon her hand.

"You want to know what passed, and perhaps it is better that you should know even if it distresses you. I sent a messenger in the motor to Sir Giles last night to tell him of your accident and to beg him to return here with him. He came back alone.

"He did not, in fact, see Sir Giles, though the message was delivered. I waited till noon today to see if he would come, and then as there was no sign of him I went myself in the motor to fetch him."

"Ah!" Anne's lips parted to utter the word. They were quivering uncontrollably.

"I saw him," Nap went on very quietly. "I

practically forced an entrance. I told him you were wanting him. I was quite kind to him, for your sake."

She fancied that his grim lips smiled.

"But I regret to say he didn't appreciate my kindness, and I soon saw that he was in no state to come to you even if he would. So, I left him and came away."

"Ah!" Again that faint exclamation that was like the half-uttered cry of a woman's heart. "He wasn't . . . wasn't rude to you, I hope?"

Nap's teeth showed for an instant. He made no reply.

"Mr. Errol," she said beseechingly, "please tell me everything! He did not . . . did not . . ."

"Kick me?" questioned Nap drily. "My dear lady, no man may kick Nap Errol and live. So I did not give him the opportunity."

She uttered a quick sob and turned her head upon the pillow. The tears were running down her face.

The hand that pressed her wrist began to rub it very gently.

"That's the worst of telling the truth," Nap said softly. "It is sure to hurt someone."

"I am glad you told me," she whispered back, "though I don't know what to say to you . . . how to atone . . ."

"I will tell you then," he answered swiftly. "Stay quietly here and be as happy as you can till the doctor gives you leave to go back. You will have to do it in any case, but, if you feel you owe me anything, which of course you don't, do it willingly—please do it willingly."

He smiled again, and his smile when free from cynicism held a wonderful charm.

She could not answer him in words, but her fingers closed upon his. Instantly she felt his answering pressure.

A moment later he laid her hand down very gently and left her.

* * *

Nap entered Anne's room with the air of one well assured of his welcome.

"Are you in a mood for chess?" he asked.

"Now, you're not to plague her, Nap," put in Mrs. Errol. "She isn't going to spend her last evening amusing you."

"Oh, please," protested Anne. "It is your son who has had all the amusing to do."

Nap smiled.

"There's for you, Alma Mater!" he remarked, as he sat down.

"Lady Carfax is much too forbearing to say anything else," retorted Mrs. Errol.

"Lady Carfax always tells the truth," said Nap, beginning to set the chess-board, "which is the exact reason why all her swains adore her."

"Well," said Mrs. Errol very deliberately, though without venom, "I guess that's about the last quality I should expect you to appreciate."

"Strange to say, it is actually the first just now," said Nap. "Are you going, Alma Mater? Don't let me drive you away!"

He rose, nevertheless, to open the door for her; and Mrs. Errol went, somewhat with the air of one complying with an unspoken desire.

Nap came softly back and resumed his task.

"P'r'aps you will be good enough to refrain from referring to me again as the august lady's son," he said. "She doesn't like it."

"Why not?" said Anne, in astonishment.

He glanced up at her as if contemplating something.

"You see, the benign mother is not over and above proud of me," he drawled. "If it were Bertie now, well, I guess even you will admit that Bertie is the flower of the flock."

His manner mystified her, but it was not her way to seek to probe mysteries. She smiled as she said:

"I have yet to discover that you are so very despicable."

"You have yet to discover many things," said Nap enigmatically. "Will you be pleased to make the first move?"

She did so silently. They had played together several times before. He had formed a habit of visiting her every evening, and it had been a welcome diversion from the constant anxiety that pressed so heavily upon her.

Nap was an expert player, yet he seemed to enjoy the poor game which was all she had to offer. Perhaps he liked to feel her at his mercy. She strongly suspected that he often deliberately prolonged the contest, though he seldom allowed her to beat him.

Tonight, however, he seemed to be in a restless mood, and she soon saw that he was bent upon a swift victory. He made his moves with a quick dexterity that baffled her completely, and but a very few minutes elapsed before he uttered his customary warning.

"You would do well to beware."

"Which means that I am beaten, I suppose," she said with a smile of resignation.

"You can save yourself if you like," he said, with his eyes on the board, "if you consider it worthwhile."

"I don't think I do," she answered. "The end will be the same."

His eyes flashed up at her.

"You surrender unconditionally?"

She continued to smile despite the sadness of her face.

"Absolutely. I am so accustomed to defeat that I am getting callous."

"You seem to have great confidence in my chivalry," he said, looking full at her.

"I have every confidence, Mr. Errol," she answered gravely. "I think that you and your brother are the most chivalrous men I know."

His laugh had a ring of harshness.

"Believe me, I am not accustomed to being ranked with the saints," he said. "How shall I get away from your halo? I warn you, it's a most awful misfit. You'll find it out presently, and make me suffer for your mistake."

"You haven't a very high opinion of my sense of justice," Anne said, with just a ring of reproach in her gentle voice.

"No," he said recklessly. "None whatever. You are sure to forget who fashioned the halo. Women always do."

Anne was silent.

He leaned suddenly towards her, careless of the chessmen that rolled in all directions.

"I haven't been living up to that halo today," he said, and there was that in his voice that touched her to quick pity. "I've been snapping and biting like a wild beast all day long. I've been in hell myself, and I've made it hell wherever I went."

"Oh, but why?"

Involuntarily she held out her hand to him as one who would assist a friend in deep waters. He took it, held it closely, bowed his forehead upon it, and so sat tensely silent.

"Something is wrong. I wish I could help you," she said at last.

He lifted his head, met her eyes of grave compassion, and abruptly set her free.

"You have done what you could for me," he said. "You've made me hate my inferno. But you can't pull me out. You have other fish to fry."

"Whatever I am doing I shall not forget my friends, Nap," she said, with great earnestness.

"No," he returned, "you won't forget them.

I shouldn't wonder if you prayed for them even. I am sure you are one of the faithful."

There was more suppressed misery than irony in his voice.

"But is that likely to help when you don't so much as know what to pray for?"

He got up and moved away from her with that noiseless footfall that was so like the stealthy padding of a beast.

Anne lay and silently watched him. Her uncertainty regarding him had long since passed away. Though she was far from understanding him, he had become an intimate friend, and she treated him as such.

True, he was unlike any other man she had ever met, but that fact ceased to embarrass her. She accepted him as he was. He came back at length and sat down, smiling at her, though somewhat grimly.

"You will pardon your poor jester," he said, "if he fails to make a joke on your last night. He could make jokes, plenty of them, but not of the sort that would please you."

Anne said nothing. She would not, if she could help it, betray to any how much she was dreading the morrow. But she felt that he knew it in spite of her.

His next words revealed the fact.

"You are going to purgatory," he said, "and I am going to perdition. Do you know, I sometimes wonder if we shouldn't do better to turn and fly in the face of the gods when they drive us too hard. Why do we give in when we've nothing to gain and all to lose?"

She met his look with her steadfast eyes.

"Does duty count as nothing?" she said.

He made an impatient movement, and would have spoken, but she stopped him.

"Please don't rail at duty. I know your creed is pleasure, but the pursuit of pleasure does not, after all, bring happiness."

"Who wants pleasure?" demanded Nap fiercely.

There fell a brief silence. Then he rose.

"I am afraid I am not fit for civilized society tonight. I will say good-bye."

He held her hand for a moment.

"You will let me see you sometimes?"

"I hope to come now and then to Baronmead," she answered quietly. "But you will not . . . please . . . come to the Manor again."

He looked down at her with eyes that had become inscrutable.

"I shall not come against your will," he said.

"Thank you," she answered simply.

And so he left her.

Chapter Three

As Dot emerged among the last of the congregation from the church on the Sunday morning following her visit to Baronmead, she found Lucas Errol leaning upon the open lynch-gate.

He greeted her with his kindly smile. But she blushed vividly at meeting him, for there in the road below, doing something to the motor, was Bertie.

The Rector joined them on the path before the house and urged his visitor to come in and see his orchids, which were in the conservatory. Be believed he had one very rare specimen.

When Bertie arrived he found his brother deep in a botanical discussion with the enthusiastic Rector.

He turned to look for Dot.

He knew his way about the lower regions of the Rectory, and he began a systematic search forthwith. She was not, however, to be very readily found. He glanced into all the downstairs rooms without success.

Then he heard her calling agitatedly for help.

He tore up the stairs with lightning speed and found her at the top of the house in an old cupboard used for storing fruit. She was mounted upon a crazy pair of steps that gave signs of imminent collapse and to save herself she was clinging to the highest shelf with both hands.

"Be quick!" she cried to him. "Be quick! I'm slipping every second!"

The words were hardly uttered before the steps gave a sudden loud crack and fell from beneath her with a crash. But in the same instant Bertie sprang in and caught her firmly round the knees. He proceeded with much presence of mind to seat her on his shoulder.

"That's all right. I've got you," he said cheerily. "None the worse, eh? What are you trying to do? May as well finish before you come down."

Dot laughed.

"I'm getting apples for dessert."

He lowered her from his shoulder to his arms with perfect ease, set her on the ground, and held her fast.

"Dot," he said, his voice sunk almost to a whisper.

"Let me go!"

But still he held her.

"Dot," he said again. "I won't hustle you any. I swear I won't hustle you. But, my dear, you'll marry me someday?"

Dot was silent. She was straining against his arms, and yet he held her, not fiercely, not passionately, but with a mastery the greater for its very coolness.

"I'll wait for you," he said. "I'll wait three years. I shall be twenty-five then, and you'll be twenty-one. But you'll marry me then, Dot. You'll have to marry me then."

"Have to!" flashed Dot.

"Yes, have to," he repeated coolly. "You are mine."

"I'm not, Bertie!" she declared indignantly. "How . . . how dare you hold me against my will? And you're upsetting the apples too. Bertie, you . . . you're horrid."

"Yes, I know," said Bertie, an odd note of soothing in his voice. "That's what you English people always do when you're beaten. You hurl insults, and go on fighting. But it's nothing but a waste of energy, and only makes the whipping the more thorough."

"You hateful American!" gasped Dot. "As if . . . as if . . . we could be beaten!"

She had struggled vainly for some seconds and was breathless. Bertie seized her wrists and drew them behind his neck.

"And yet you love me," he said. "You love yourself better, but you love me."

His face was bent to hers, and he looked closely into her eyes. And perhaps it was something in his look that moved her, perhaps it was only the realisation of her own utter impotence, but Dot suddenly hid her face upon his shoulder and began to cry.

His arms were about her in an instant. He held her against his heart.

"My dearest, have I been a brute to you? I only wanted to make you understand. Say, Dot, don't cry, dear, don't cry!"

"I . . . I'm not!" sobbed Dot.

"Of course not," he agreed. "Anyone can see that. But still, darling, don't!"

Dot recovered herself with surprising rapidity.

"Bertie, you . . . you're a great big donkey!" She confronted him with wet, accusing eyes. "What you said just now wasn't true, and if . . . if you're a gentleman you'll apologise."

"I'll let you kick me all the way downstairs if you like," said Bertie contritely. "I didn't mean to hurt you, honest I didn't mean to make you . . ."

"You didn't!" broke in Dot. "But you didn't tell the truth. That's why I'm angry with you. You told a lie."

"I?" said Bertie.

"Yes, you!" said Dot.

"What did I say?" asked Bertie, hastily casting back his thoughts.

"You said," she spoke with immense deliberation, "that I loved myself best."

"Well?" said Bertie.

"Well," she said, and took up her basket as one on the point of departure, "it wasn't true. There!"

"Dot!" His hand was on the basket too. He stopped her without touching her. "Dot!"

Dot's eyes began to soften, a dimple showing suddenly near the corner of her mouth.

"You shouldn't tell lies, Bertie," she said.

And that was the last remark she made for several seconds, but later she said breathlessly:

"Your family will not want me to . . . marry you."

"They love you already."

"Not Nap!"

"Nap doesn't matter!"

"He does . . . he told someone, I heard him, that I was after your money!"

There was a sob in Dot's voice. Bertie took her in his arms.

"Damn Nap," he exclaimed. "He is jealous! I know you love me and that is all that matters."

He kissed her but Dot was still uneasy.

* * *

Lucas Errol was entertaining a large house-party and the great hall was full of guests. The hubbub of voices was considerable, but when Mrs. Errol spoke everyone listened.

"Where do you think I've just come from?" she asked.

"You've been bearding the lion in his den," Nap answered. "And not unsuccessfully, to judge by appearances. In other words, you've been to the Manor and have drunk tea with the lord thereof."

Mrs. Errol subsided into the chair and looked round upon her interested audience.

"Yes, I've been to the Manor. I've had tea with Anne Carfax. And I've talked to the Squire. He was pretty mad at first, but I kept on hammering it into him till even he began to get tired."

She smiled.

"I was mighty kind on the whole. But I guess he isn't under any misapprehension as to what I think of him. And I'm going over tomorrow to fetch dear Anne over here to lunch."

With which cheerful announcement Mrs. Errol picked up a cup of tea and drank it with a triumphant air.

"I told him," she resumed, "he'd better watch his reputation, for he was beginning to be regarded as the local Bluebeard."

"It must have been real edifying for Lady Carfax," drawled Nap.

Mrs. Errol turned upon him.

"I'm no bigger a fool than I look, Nap. Lady Carfax didn't hear a word. We had it out in the park. He was pretty near speechless by the time

I'd done with him, but he did just manage at parting to call me an impertinent old woman. And I called him . . . a gentleman!"

Mrs. Errol paused.

"I was wheezing myself by that time," she concluded. "But I had my say. Why, it's five weeks now since Anne left, and she's only been over once in all that time, and then, I gather, there was such a row that she didn't feel like facing another."

"An infernal shame!" declared Bertie hotly. "I'll drive you over myself tomorrow to fetch her. We'll get up some sports in her honour. I'm sure she likes tobogganing."

"I wonder if she will come," murmured Nap.

"She'll come," Mrs. Errol said with finality.

Though it was nearly the middle of March there had been a heavy fall of snow, and a continuous frost succeeding it had turned Baronmead into an Alpine paradise.

Tobogganing and skating filled the hours of each day; dancing made fly the hours of each night. Strings of fairy lights were being arranged and Chinese lanterns bobbed in every bush.

Bertie was deeply engrossed in these preparations, but he tore himself away to drive his mother to the Manor on the following morning.

His alacrity to do this was explained when he told her that he wanted to drop into the Rectory and persuade the Rector to bring Dot that night to see the fun.

Lucas, leaning upon Nap's shoulder, went

down to the lake to watch the skaters and to superintend Bertie's preparations for the evening's entertainment.

He seated himself on a stone bench that overlooked the lake. His eyes followed the darting figures of the skaters with a certain intentness. Nap leaned upon the balustrade and watched him.

"Why don't you see Capper again?" he asked suddenly.

"I am afraid he is on the wrong side of the Atlantic," Lucas replied.

"You can cable to him."

"Yes, I know." Slowly Lucas raised his eyes to his brother's face. "I can have him over to tell me what he told me before—that I haven't the recuperative strength essential to make his double operation a success."

"He may tell you something different this time."

Lucas was silent.

"Say, Lucas"—there was more than insistence in his tone this time; it held compulsion—"you aren't faint-hearted?"

The blue eyes began to smile.

"I think not, Boney. But I've got to hang on for the present, till you and the boy are married. P'r'aps then I'll take the risk."

Nap looked supercilious.

"And if it is not my intention to marry?"

"You must marry, my dear fellow. You'll never be satisfied otherwise."

"You think marriage the hall-mark of respectability?" Nap sneered openly.

"I think," Lucas answered quietly, "that for you marriage is the only end. The love of a good woman would be your salvation. And you know it."

It was nearly a minute later before Nap spoke, and by that time the humming of an approaching motor was clearly audible.

"It may be the truth," he said, in a tone as deliberate as his brother's, "and it may not. But no good woman will ever marry me, Luke. And I shall never marry anything else."

He stooped, offering his shoulder for support.

"And if you won't send for Capper—I shall."

The two brothers were standing together on the steps when Anne alighted from the car, and her first thought as she moved towards them was of their utter dissimilarity.

They might have been men of different nationalities, so essentially unlike each other were they in every detail. And yet she felt for both that ready friendship that sprung from warmest gratitude.

Nap kept her hand a moment in his grasp while he looked at her with that bold stare of his that she had never yet desired to avoid. On the occasion of her last visit to Baronmead they had not met.

She wondered if he was about to upbraid her for neglecting her friends, but he said nothing, leaving it to Lucas to inquire after her health while he stood by and watched her with those dusky, intent eyes of his that seemed to miss nothing.

"I am quite strong again, thank you," she said, in answer to her host's kindly questioning. "And you, Mr. Errol?"

"I am getting strong too." He smiled. "I am almost equal to running alone; but doubtless you are past that stage. Slow and sure has been my motto for some years now."

"It is a very good one," said Anne, in that gentle voice which was like the voice of a girl.

He heard the sympathy in it, and his eyes softened; but he passed the matter by.

"I hope you have come to stay. Has my mother managed to persuade you?"

"She will spend tonight anyway," said Mrs. Errol.

"And only tonight," said Anne, wtih quiet firmness. "You are all very kind, but . . ."

"We want you," interposed Lucas Errol.

She smiled, a quick smile that seemed reminiscent of happier days.

"Yes, and thank you for it. But I must return in good time tomorrow. I told my husband that I would do so. He is spending the night in town, but he will be back tomorrow."

Nap's teeth were visible, hard clenched upon his lower lip as he listened, but still he said nothing. There was something peculiarly forcible, even sinister, in his silence.

Not until Anne presently turned and directly addressed him did his attitude change.

"Will you take me to see the lake?" she said. "It looked so charming as we drove up."

He moved instantly to accompany her. They went out together into the hard brightness of the winter morning.

"It is so good to be here," Anne said, a little wistfully. "It is like a day in paradise."

He laughed at that, not very pleasantly.

"It is indeed," she persisted, "except for one thing. Now tell me: how have I offended?"

"You, Lady Carfax?"

His brows met for an instant in a single, savage line.

"Is it only my fancy?" she said. "I have a feeling that all is not peace."

He stopped abruptly by the balustrade that bounded the terrace.

"The Queen can do no wrong," he said. "She can hurt, but she cannot offend."

"Then how have I hurt you, Nap?" she said.

The quiet dignity of the question demanded an answer, but it was slow in coming. Anne waited quite motionless beside him. She was not looking at the skaters; her eyes had gone beyond them.

"I am a fool to take you to task for snubbing me," he said. "But I am not accustomed to being snubbed. Let that be my excuse."

"Please tell me what you mean," said Anne.

He looked at her.

"Do you tell me you do not know?"

Her clear eyes met his.

"Why should I snub you? I thought you were a friend."

"A friend," he said, with emphasis. "I thought so too. But . . ."

"Yes?" she said gently.

"Isn't it customary with you to answer your friends when they write to you?" he asked.

Her expression changed. A look of sharp pain showed for an instant in her eyes.

"My invariable custom, Nap," she said very steadily.

"Then, that letter of mine . . ." He paused.

"When did you write it?"

"On the evening of the day you came here last, the day I missed you."

"It did not reach me," she said, her voice very low.

"I sent it by messenger," he said. "I was hunting that day. I sat down and wrote the moment I heard you had been. Tawny Hudson took it."

"It did not reach me," she repeated. She was very pale; her eyes had dropped from his.

"I was going to allow you a month to answer that letter," he went on, as though she had not spoken. "After that our friendship would have been at an end. The month will be up tomorrow."

Anne was silent.

"Lady Carfax," he said, "will you swear to me that you never received that letter?"

"No," she said.

"You will not?"

"I will not."

He made a sudden movement, such a movement as a man makes involuntarily at an unexpected dart of pain.

Anne raised her eyes very quietly.

"Let us be quite honest," she said. "No oath is ever necessary between friends."

"You expect me to believe you?" he said, and his voice was shaken by some emotion he scarcely tried to hide.

She smiled very faintly.

"You do believe me."

He turned sharply from her.

"Let us go down," he said.

At Bertie's persuasion Anne went down with him to the lake in the afternoon, where they skated together till sunset.

She had a curious feeling that Nap was watching her the whole time, though he was nowhere to be seen; nor did he appear at tea in the great hall.

Anne had brought no fancy dress, but her hostess was eager to provide for her. She clothed her in a white domino and black velvet mask, and insisted upon her wearing a splendid diamond tiara in the shape of a heart in her soft hair.

When she finally descended the stairs in Mrs. Errol's company, a slim man dressed as a harlequin in black and silver was waiting for her halfway down. He bowed low and presented her with a glorious spray of crimson roses, with the words:

"For the Queen, who can do no wrong!"

"My, Nap! How you startled me!" ejaculated Mrs. Errol.

But Anne said nothing. She only looked him straight in the eyes for an instant, and passed on with the roses in her hand.

After dinner when they went out at last onto the terrace, the whole garden was transformed into a paradise of glowing colours. The lake shone like a prism of glass, and over all the stars hung as if suspended very near the earth.

Anne stood by Lucas and watched the gay scene silently.

"You ought to be skating," he said presently.

She shook her head.

"Not yet. I like watching. It makes me think of when I was a girl."

"Not very long ago," said the cool voice of a skater who had just glided up.

Anne started a little, but Lucas scarcely moved.

"Lady Carfax is waiting to go on the ice," he said.

"And I am waiting to take her," the newcomer said.

His slim, graceful figure in its black, tight-fitting garb sparkled at every turn. His eyes shone through his velvet mask like the eyes of an animal in the dark.

He glided nearer and held out his hands to Anne, but for some reason inexplicable to herself, Anne stepped back.

"I don't think I will skate yet," she said. "I am quite happy where I am."

"You will be happier with me," said the harlequin, with imperial confidence.

He waved his hand to Hudson, standing a few paces away with her skates, took them from him, and motioned her to the bank.

She stepped forward, not very willingly. Hudson, at another sign, spread a rug for her. She sat down, and the glittering harlequin kneeled upon the ice before her and fastened the blades to her feet.

It took only a couple of minutes; he was deft in all his ways. And then he was on his feet again, and with a royal gesture he helped her to hers.

Anne looked at him half dazzled. The shimmering figure seemed to be decked in diamonds.

"Are you ready?" he said.

She looked into the glowing eyes and felt as if some magic attraction were drawing her against her will.

"Take care of her, Boney," Lucas admonished.

In another moment they were gliding into that prism of many lights and colours, and the harlequin, holding Anne's hands, laughed enigmatically as he sped her away.

It seemed to Anne that she had left the earth altogether, and was gliding upwards through starland without effort or conscious movement of any sort, simply as though lifted by the hands that held her own.

Their vitality thrilled through her like a strong current of electricity. She felt that whichever way they turned, wherever they led her, she must be safe. There was a quivering ecstasy in that dazzling, rapid rush that filled her veins like liquid fire.

"Do you know where you are?" he asked her once.

"I feel as if I were caught in a rainbow," she answered in a species of breathless rapture.

He laughed again at that, a soft, exultant laugh, and drew her more swiftly on.

They left the other masqueraders behind; they left the shimmering lake and its many lights; and at last in the starlight only they slackened speed.

The full moon was just rising over a long silver ridge of down. She stood with her face to its cold splendour, her hands still locked in that vital grip.

Slowly at last, compelled she knew not how, she turned to the man beside her.

His eyes were blazing at her with a lurid fire, and suddenly that sensation that had troubled her once before in his presence, a sensation of sharp uneasiness, pricked through her confidence.

She stood quite still, conscious of a sudden quickening of her heart. But she did not shrink from that burning gaze. She met it with level eyes.

For seconds they stood so, facing each other. He seemed to be trying in some fashion to subjugate her, to beat her down; but she would not yield an inch. And it was he who finally broke the spell.

"Am I forgiven?"

"For what?" she said.

"For pretending to disbelieve you this morning."

"Was it pretence?" she asked.

"No, it wasn't!" he told her fiercely. "It was deadly earnest. I would have given all I had to be able to disbelieve you. Do you know that?"

"But why, Nap?"

"Why?" he said. "Because your goodness and your purity are making a slave of me. If I could catch you, if I could catch you only once—cheating, as all other women cheat, I should be free. But you are irreproachable and incorruptible. I believe you are above temptation."

"Oh, you don't know me," she interposed quietly. "But even if I were all these things, why should it vex you?"

"Why?" he said. "Because you hold me back, you check me at every turn. You harness me to your chariot wheels, and I have to run in the path of virtue whether I will or not!"

He broke off with a laugh that had in it a note of savagery.

"Don't you even care to know what was in that letter that you never had?" he asked abruptly.

"Tell me!" she said.

"I told you that I was mad to have missed you that day. I begged you to let me have a line before you came again. I besought you to let me call upon you and to fix a day. I signed myself your humble and devoted slave, Napoleon Errol."

He ceased, still laughing queerly, with his lower lip between his teeth. Anne stood silent for many seconds.

"You must never come to see me," she said very decidedly.

"Not if I bring the mother as a chaperon?" he jested.

"Neither you nor your mother must ever come to see me again," she said firmly. "And, Nap, though I know that the writing of that letter meant nothing whatever to you, I am more sorry than I can say that you sent it."

He threw back his head arrogantly.

"What?" he said. "Has the Queen no further use for her jester? Am I not even to write to you then?"

"I think not."

"And why?" he demanded imperiously.

"I think you know why."

"Do I know why? Is it because you are afraid of your husband?"

"No."

"Afraid of me then?"

There was almost a taunt in the words.

"No," she said again.

"Why, then?"

He was looking full into her eyes. There was something peculiarly sinister about his masked face. She almost felt as if he were menacing her.

"For a reason that means much to me, though it may not appeal to you. Because my husband is not always sane, and I am afraid of what he might do to you if he were provoked any further."

"Great Lucifer!" said Nap. "Does he think I make love to you then?"

"He is not always sane," she repeated.

"You are right," he said. "That reason does

not appeal to me. Your husband's hallucinations are not worth considering. But I don't propose on that account to write any more letters for his edification. For the future . . ."

"For the future," Anne interrupted, "there must be no correspondence between us at all. I know it seems unreasonable to you, but that cannot be helped. Mr. Errol, surely you are generous enough, chivalrous enough, to understand."

"No, I don't understand," Nap said. "I don't understand how you can, by the widest stretch of the imagination, believe it your duty to conform to the caprices of a maniac."

"How can I help it?" she said very sadly.

He was silent for a moment. His hands were still gripping hers; she could feel her wedding ring being forced into her flesh.

"Like our mutual friend, Major Shirley," he said slowly, "I wonder why you stick to the man."

She turned her face away with a sound that was almost a moan.

"You never loved him," he said with conviction.

She was silent. Yet after a little, as he waited, she spoke as one compelled.

"I live with him because he gave me that for which I married him. He fulfilled his part of the bargain. I must fulfil mine. I was nothing but his bailiff's daughter, remember; a bailiff who had robbed him, for whose escape from penal servitude I paid the price."

"Great heavens!" said Nap.

She turned to him quickly, with an impulsiveness that was almost girlish.

"I have never told anyone else. I tell you because I know you are my friend and because I want you to understand. We will never, please, speak of it again."

"Wait!" Nap's voice rang stern. "Was it part of the bargain that he should insult you, trample on you, make you lead a dog's life without a single friend to make it bearable?"

"Let us go back."

He wheeled at once, still holding her hands. They skated a few yards in silence. Then suddenly, almost under his breath, he spoke.

"I am not going to give up my friendship with you. Let that be clearly understood."

"You are very good to me," she said simply.

"No, I am not. I am human, that's all. I don't think this state of affairs can last much longer."

She shuddered. Her husband's condition had been very much worse of late, but she did not tell him so.

They were skating rapidly back towards the head of the lake. In front of them sounded the swirling rush of skates and the laughter of many voices.

"I'm sorry I've been unkind to you," Nap said abruptly. "You mustn't mind me. It's just my way."

"Oh, I don't mind you, Nap," she answered gently.

And with that he stooped suddenly and shot forward like a meteor, bearing her with him.

They flashed back into the gay throng of masqueraders, and mingled with the crowd as if they had never left it.

* * *

As Anne sped along through the sunshine on that winter day she found leisure from her cares to enjoy the swift journey in the great, luxurious car. The burden she carried perpetually weighed less heavily upon her than usual.

She thought of Nap with anxiety. She was sure he had not intended to let her go without farewell, but she hoped earnestly that he would not pursue her to the Manor to tell her so.

Her husband must have intercepted his letter. He had doubtless read it and been inflamed by it.

Hating her himself, yet he was fiercely jealous of her friends, these new friends of hers who had lavished upon her every kindness in her time of need, to whom she must always feel warmly grateful.

She knew that a visit from Nap would place her in an intolerable position, and with all her heart she hoped that her caution of the previous day had taken effect.

But she was sorry, unquestionably she was sorry, to have left without bidding him farewell. It might be a long time before they would meet again.

With the thought yet in her mind she looked out the window in front of her, and saw his slim, supple figure, clad in a white sweater, shoot swiftly down a snow-draped slope ahead of her, like a meteor flashing earthwards out of the blue.

His arms were extended; his movements had a lithe grace that was irresistibly fascinating to the eye. Slight though he was, he might have been a young god descended on a shaft of sunshine from Olympus.

But the thought that darted all unbidden through Anne's mind was of something far different.

She banished it on the instant with startled precipitancy; but it left a scar behind that burned like the sudden searing of a hot iron.

"I beheld Satan as lightning fall from heaven."

The car was stopping. The figure on skis was waiting motionless by the roadside. It ran smoothly up to her and stopped.

"Dramatic, wasn't it?" smiled Nap. "Did you think you were going to escape without another word?"

"I had almost begun to think so," she admitted, smiling also.

He stooped to take off the skis, then stepped to the door. He leaned towards her. There was no faintest sign of cynicism in his face that day. He was in the mood of good comradeship in which she liked him best.

"Walk across to the park with me," he said. "It is scarcely a mile by the downs. The man can go on to the Manor with your things and wait here for me on his way back."

Anne considered for a moment, but only for a moment. It might make her late for the luncheon hour, but she was convinced that her husband would not return before the evening.

And the world was very enchanting that winter day. The very ground was scattered with diamonds.

"Yes, I will come," she said.

He handed her out, and picked up his discarded skis. His dark face smiled with a certain triumph. The grim lines about his mouth were less apparent than usual. He moved with the elastic swing of well-knitted limbs.

Anne went over the hill with him, feeling that she had snatched one more hour in paradise.

* * *

By what magic he cajoled her into trying her skill upon skis Anne never afterwards remembered. It seemed to her later that the exhilarating atmosphere of that cloudless winter day must have in some magic fashion revived in her the youth which had been crushed out of existence so long ago.

A strange, irresponsible happiness possessed her, so new, so subtly sweet, that the heavy burden she had borne for so long seemed almost to have shrunk into insignificance.

She forgot the seven dreary years that separated her from her girlhood, forgot the bondage to which she was returning.

It was like an enchanting dream to her, a dream through which she lived with all the greater zest because it so soon must pass.

All the pent energies of her vanished youth

were in the dream. She could not, for that once she could not, deny them vent.

And Nap, strung to a species of fierce gaiety that she had never seen in him before, urged her perpetually on. He would not let her pause to think, but yet he considered her at every turn.

He scoffed like a boy at her efforts to ski, but he held her up strongly while he scoffed, taking care of her with that adroitness that marked everything he did. And while they thus dallied the time passed swiftly, more swiftly than either realized.

The sun began to draw to the southwest. The diamonds ceased to sparkle save here and there obliquely. The haze of a winter afternoon settled upon the downs.

Suddenly Anne noticed these things, suddenly the shining garment of her youth slipped from her, and left her like Cinderella when the spell of her enchantment was broken.

"Nap!" she exclaimed. "I must go! I must have been dreaming to forget the time!"

"Time!" laughed Nap. "What is time?"

"It is something that I have to remember," she said. "Why, it must be nearly two o'clock!"

Nap glanced at the sun and made no comment. Anne felt for and consulted her watch. It was already three.

She looked up in amazement and dismay.

"I must go at once!"

"Don't!" said Nap. "I am sure your watch is wrong."

"I must go at once," she repeated firmly. "It is

long past the luncheon hour. I had no idea we had been here so long. You must go too. Your chauffeur will think you are never coming."

The skis were still on her feet. Nap looked at her speculatively.

"This is rather an abrupt end," he said. "Won't you have one more go? A few minutes more or less can't make any difference now."

"They may make all the difference," Anne said. "Really, I ought not."

They stood on a gentle slope that led downwards to the path she must take.

"Just ski down into the valley from here then," urged Nap. "It's quicker than walking. I won't hold you this time. You won't fall."

The suggestion was reasonable, and the fascination of the sport had taken firm hold of her. Anne smiled, and yielded. She set her feet together and let herself go.

Almost at the same instant, a sound that was like the bellow of an infuriated bull reached her from above.

She tried to turn, but the skis were already slipping over the snow. To preserve her balance she was forced to go, and for seconds that seemed like hours she slid down the hillside, her heart thumping in her throat; her nerves straining and twitching to check that maddening progress. For she knew that sound.

She had heard it before, had shrunk secretly many a time before its coarse brutality. It was the yell of a man in headlong, furious wrath, an animal yell, unreasoning, hideously bestial; and she feared, feared horribly, what that yell might portend.

She reached the valley, and managed to swerve round without falling. But for an instant she could not, she dared not, raise her eyes.

Clear on the frosty air came sounds that made her blood turn cold. She felt as if her heart would suffocate her. A brief blindness blotted out all things.

Then with an agonized effort she forced back her weakness, she forced herself to look. Yes, the thing she had feared so horribly was being enacted like a ghastly nightmare above her.

There on the slope was her husband, a gigantic figure outlined against the snow. He had not stopped to parley. Those mad fits of passion always deprived him at the outset of the few reasoning powers that yet remained to him.

Without question or explanation of any kind he had flung himself upon the man he deemed his enemy, and Anne now beheld him, gripping him by the neck as a terrier grips a rat, and flogging him with the loaded crop he always carried to the hunt.

Nap was writhing to and fro like an eel, striving, she saw, to overthrow his adversary. But the gigantic strength of madness was too great for his lithe activity. By sheer weight he was borne down.

With an anguished cry Anne started to intervene. But two steps with the skis flung her headlong upon the snow, and while she struggled vainly to rise, she heard the awful blows above her like pistol-shots through the stillness.

Once she heard a curse, and once a demoniacal laugh, and once, thrilling her through and through, spurring her to wilder efforts, a dreadful sound that was like the cry of a stricken animal.

She gained her feet at last, and again started on her upward way. Nap had been forced to his knees, but he was still fighting fiercely, as a rat will fight to the last. She cried to him wildly that she was coming, was coming, made three paces, only to trip and fall again.

Then she knew that, so handicapped, she could never reach them, and with shaking, fumbling fingers she set herself to unfasten the straps that bound the skis.

It took her a long, long time, all the longer for her fevered haste. And still that awful, flail-like sound went on and on, though all sound of voices had wholly ceased.

Free at last, she stumbled to her feet, and tore madly up the hill. She saw as she went that Nap was not struggling any longer.

He was hanging like a wet rag from the merciless grip that upheld him, and though his limp body seemed to shudder at every crashing blow, he made no voluntary movement of any sort.

As she drew near, her husband suddenly swung round as though aware of her, and dropped him. He fell in a huddled heap upon the snow, and lay, twisted, motionless as a dead thing.

Sir Giles, his eyes suffused and terrible, turned upon his wife.

"There lies your gallant lover!" he snarled at her. "I think I've cured him of his fancy for you."

Her eyes met his. For a single instant, hatred, unveiled, passionate, shone out at him like sudden, darting lightning.

For a single instant she dared him with the courage born of hatred. It was a challenge so distinct and personal, so fierce, that he, satiated for the moment with revenge, drew back instinctively before it, as an animal shrinks from the flame.

She uttered not a word. She did not after that one scorching glance deign to do battle with him. Without a gesture she dismissed him, kneeling beside his vanquished foe.

Sir Giles turned and tramped heavily away. Anne did not watch him go. It was nothing to her at the moment whether he went or stayed.

She knelt beside the huddled, unconscious figure and tried to straighten the crumpled limbs. The sweater had been literally torn from his back, and the shirt beneath it was in blood-stained tatters.

His face was covered with blood. Sir Giles had not been particular as to where the whip had fallen. Great purple welts crossed and recrossed each other on the livid features.

The bleeding lips were drawn back in a devilish grimace. He looked as if he had been terribly mauled by some animal.

Anne gripped a handful of snow, hardly

knowing what she did, and tried to stanch the blood that ran from an open cut on his temple.

She was not trembling any longer. The emergency had steadied her. But the agony of those moments was worse than any she had ever known before.

Minutes passed. She was beginning to despair. An icy dread was at her heart. He lay so lifeless, so terribly inert. She had attempted to lift him, but the dead weight was too much for her.

She could only rest his head against her, and wipe away the blood that trickled persistently from that dreadful, sneering mouth.

Would he ever speak again? she asked herself. Were the fiery eyes fast shut forever? Was he dead—he whose vitality had always held her like a charm? Had her friendship done this for him, that friendship he had valued so highly?

She stooped lower over him. The anguish of the thought was more than she could bear.

"O, God," she prayed suddenly and passionately, "don't let him die! Don't let him die!"

And in that moment Nap's eyes opened wide and fixed themselves upon her.

He did not attempt to move or speak, but the snarling look went wholly out of his face. The thin lips met and closed over the battered mouth. He lay regarding her intently, as if he were examining some curious thing he had never seen before.

And before that gaze Anne's eyes wavered and sank. She felt she could never meet his look again.

"Are you better?" she whispered. "Can I . . . will you let me . . . help you?"

"No," he said. "Just leave me!"

He spoke quite quietly, but the very sound of his voice sent a perfect storm of emotion through her.

"I can't!" she said almost fiercely. "I won't! Let me help you! Let me do what I can!"

He stirred a little, and his brow contracted, but he never took his eyes from her face.

"Don't be upset," he said, with an effort. "I'm not going—to die!"

"Tell me what to do," she urged piteously. "Can I lift you a little higher?"

"For heaven's sake—no!" he said, and swallowed a shudder. "My collar-bone's broken."

He was silent for a space, but still his dusky eyes watched her perpetually.

"Let me hold your hand," he said.

She put it into his, and he held it tightly. The blood was running down his face again, and she wiped it softly away.

"Thank you," he said.

Those two words, spoken almost under his breath, had a curious effect upon her. She felt as if something had suddenly entered and pierced her heart. Before she knew it, a sharp sob escaped her, and then all in a moment she broke down.

"Oh, Nap, Nap," she sobbed, "I wish I had died before this could happen!"

She felt his hand tighten as she crouched there beside him in her anguish, and presently she knew that he had somehow managed to raise himself to a sitting posture.

Through her agony his voice came to her. It was pitched very low, yet she heard it.

"Don't cry, for pity's sake! I shall get over it. I shall live—to get back—my own."

Torn by emotion as she was, something in the last words, spoken in that curious undertone, struck her with a subtle force. With a desperate effort she controlled herself.

She knew that he was still watching her with that strange intensity that she could not bring herself to meet. His right hand still held hers with quivering tenacity; the other trailed uselessly on the snow.

"Let me help you," she urged again.

He was silent; she feared he was going to refuse. And then she saw that his head had begun to droop forward, and realized that he was on the verge of another collapse.

Instinctively she slipped her arm about his shoulders, supporting him. He was shuddering all over. She drew his head to rest against her.

"It's the collar-bone that hurts so infernally. Could you push something under my left arm to hold it up?" he asked. "Your muff would do. Mind my wrist, that's broken too."

She heard the breath whistle sharply between his lips as with the utmost care she compiled with these instructions, but almost instantly he went on.

"Don't be afraid of touching me, unless I'm

too monstrous to touch. But I don't believe I can walk."

"I will help you," she said. "I am very strong."

"You are wonderful," he said.

And the words comforted her subtly though she did not know exactly what he meant by them.

Thereafter they scarcely spoke at all. By slow degrees he recovered his self-command, though she knew with only too keen a perception how intolerable was the pain that racked his whole body.

With her assistance and with strenuous effort he managed at last to get upon his feet, but he was immediately assailed afresh by deadly faintness, and for minutes he could only stand by means of her arms upholding him.

Later, with his one available arm across her shoulders, he essayed to walk, but it was so ghastly an ordeal that he could only accomplish a few steps at a time.

Anne did not falter now. She was past that stage. All her nerves were strung to meet his pressing need. Again and again as he hung upon her, half-fainting, she stopped to support him more adequately till he had fought down his exhaustion and was ready to struggle on again.

She remained steadfast and resolute throughout the long-drawn-out agony of that walk over the snow.

"Great Heaven!" he muttered once. "That you should do this for me!"

And she answered him quickly and passionately, as though indeed there were something within that spoke for her.

"I would do anything for you, Nap."

It was drawing near to sunset when at last the end of the journey came in sight. Anne perceived the car waiting in the distance close to the spot where Nap had descended upon her that morning.

She breathed a sigh of thankfulness.

"I scarcely thought he would have waited for you so long," she said.

"He daren't do otherwise," said Nap, and she caught a faint echo of arrogance in the words.

And then of his own free will he paused and faced her.

"You are coming with me," he said.

She shook her head.

"No, Nap."

His eyes blazed redly. His disfigured face was suddenly devilish.

"You are mad if you go back."

"No, I know what I am doing. And I am going back now. But I will come to Baronmead in the morning."

He looked at her.

"Are you—tired of life?" he asked abruptly.

She smiled, a piteous smile.

"Very, very tired!" she said. "But you needn't be afraid of that. He will not touch me. He will not even see me tonight. I know exactly what I am doing. Believe me, I am in no danger."

He gave in, seeing that she was not to be

moved from her purpose. They went a few yards farther.

"In heaven's name, come early to Baronmead," he said jerkily. "I shall have no peace till you come."

"I will," she promised.

The chauffeur came to meet them with clumsy solicitude as they neared the car, but Nap kept him at a distance.

"Don't touch me! I've had a bad fall skiing. It's torn me to ribbons. Just open the door. Lady Carfax will do the rest!"

As the man turned to obey, he murmured:

"Not a very likely story, but it will serve our turn."

"Thank you," she said very earnestly.

He did not look at her again. She had a feeling that he kept his eyes from her by a deliberate effort of the will.

Silently she helped him into the car, saw him sink back with her muff still supporting his injured arm, whispered a low "Good-bye!" and turned to the waiting chauffeur.

"Drive him quickly home," she said. "And then go for a doctor."

Not till the car was out of sight did she realise that her knees were shaking and refusing to support her.

She tottered to a gate by the roadside, and there, clinging weakly with her head bowed upon her arms, she remained for a very long time.

* * *

It was growing dusk when Anne at length came to the Manor. She was utterly weary and faint from lack of food. The servant who admitted her looked at her strangely as if half afraid.

Mechanically she bathed her face and hands and passed into her sitting-room, where her tea awaited her. Entering, she found, somewhat to her surprise, old Dimsdale waiting to serve her.

"Thank you," she said. "I can help myself."

The tea revived her, and after a little she turned her head and looked up at him.

"What is it, Dimsdale?"

Dimsdale coughed.

"It was about Sir Giles that I wanted to speak to Your Ladyship."

"Well?" she said again.

"Sir Giles, My Lady, is not himself, not at all himself. I was wondering just before you came in if I didn't ought to send for the doctor."

"Why, Dimsdale?" Anne looked straight up in to the old man's troubled face.

"It's not the same as usual, My Lady. I've never seen him like this before. There's something, I don't rightly know what, about him that fair scares me. If Your Ladyship will only let me send for the doctor . . ."

He paused.

"I don't think the doctor would be at home," she said at last. "Wait till the morning, Dimsdale, unless he is really ill."

"My Lady, it's not that," said Dimsdale. "There's nothing ails his body. But—but—it's his mind, if I may make so bold as to say it. I don't believe as he's safe, I'm afraid he'll be doing a mischief to someone."

His pause was not lost upon Anne.

"To whom, Dimsdale?" she asked.

"My Lady . . ." the old man murmured unwillingly.

"To me?" she questioned, in a quiet, unmoved voice. "Why are you afraid of that?"

Dimsdale hesitated before he said:

"He's been cutting Your Ladyship's portraits into strips and burning 'em in the study fire. It was dreadful to see him, so intent like and quiet. I saw him put his hand right into the flame once, and he didn't seem to know.

"And he came in in one of his black moods with his hunting-crop broken right in two. Carrying the pieces he was, and glaring like as if all the world was against him. I was afraid there would be trouble when he came home to lunch and found Your Ladyship not there."

He stopped, arrested by a sudden movement from Anne. She had leaned forward and covered her face with her hands. He waited silently, and presently Anne lifted her head.

"I think you must leave the matter till the morning, Dimsdale," she said. "It could do no good to have the doctor at this hour. Besides, I doubt if he could come. And Sir Giles will be himself again after a night's rest."

"I'm very much afraid not, My Lady," said Dimsdale lugubriously. "He's drinking brandy, neat brandy, all the while. I've never seen him drink like that before. It fair scares me, and that's the truth."

"You are not afraid on your own account?" Anne asked.

"Oh, no, My Lady. He wouldn't interfere with me. It's Your Ladyship . . ."

"Ah, well," she said, quietly interrupting. "you need not be afraid for me either. I shall not go downstairs again tonight. He will not be expecting me."

"Very good, My Lady."

She sat for a long time thinking of the past; then, hearing a sound at the door, she turned.

A white-faced servant stood on the threshold.

"If you please, My Lady, your coat is in a dreadful state. I was afraid there must have been an accident."

Anne stared at the woman for a few seconds with the dazed eyes of one suddenly awakened.

"Yes," she said slowly at length. "There was . . . an accident. Mr. Nap Errol was . . . hurt while skiing."

"What had I better do with the coat, My Lady?" she asked.

"Take it away!" she said sharply. "Do what you like with it! I never want to see it again."

"Very good, My Lady."

The woman withdrew, and Anne covered her face with her hands, and shuddered from head to foot.

Some time later Anne seated herself at her

writing-table. The idea of writing to her husband had come to her as an inspiration.

Then a slight sound in the passage brought her out of her reverie. She glanced up. It was probably Dimsdale. She would give him the note to deliver to his master in the morning. She crossed to the door and opened it.

The next instant, in amazement, she drew back. On the threshold, face to face with her, stood her husband!

He did not give her time to speak, but pushed straight forward into the room as if in haste. His face was white and purple in patches. His eyes were narrowed and furtive. There was something unspeakably evil in the way they avoided hers. He carried his right hand behind him.

He began to speak at once in quick, staccato tones, with which she was utterly unfamiliar.

"So you think you are going to escape me, do you? But you won't! No, not for all the Errols in the world!"

She did not answer him. There was something so utterly unusual in this abrupt visitation that she knew not how to cope with it. But he scarcely waited for an answer. He swung the door behind him with a bang.

"Do you remember," he said, his staccato tone merging into one of rising violence, "a promise I made to you the first time I caught that scoundrel making love to you? I swore that if it happened again I'd thrash him.

"Well, I'm a man who keeps his promises. I've

kept that one. And now it's your turn. I thought at first I'd kill you. But I fancy this will hurt you more."

His hand shot suddenly out from behind him, and there followed the whistle of a thong, the thick leather thong with which he kept his dogs in order.

It struck her as she stood before him, struck and curled about her shoulders, with a searing, scalding agony that turned her sick, wringing from her a cry that would never have been uttered had she been prepared.

But before he could strike again she was ready to cope with his madness. On the instant she sprang, not from him, but to him, clasping his arms with both of hers.

"Giles!" she said, and her voice rang clear and commanding. "You are not yourself. You don't know what you are doing. Look at me! Do you hear? Look at me!"

That was his vulnerable point, and instinctively she knew it. He was afraid, as a wild animal is afraid, of the compulsion of her eyes. But he fought with her savagely, furiously, refusing to face her, struggling with inarticulate oaths to break away from her clinging arms.

And Anne was powerless against him, powerless as Nap had been earlier in the day, to make any impression against his frenzied strength. She was as impotent as a child in that awful grip, and in a very few seconds she knew it.

He had already wrung his arm free and raised it to strike a second blow, while she shut her eyes in anguished expectation, still clingly blindly to his coat, when the door burst open with a crash and Dimsdale tore into the room.

Anne heard his coming but she could not turn. She was waiting with every nerve stretched and quivering for the thong to fall, when Dimsdale, with a strength abnormal for his years, flung himself at the upraised arm and bore it downwards.

She relaxed her hold and tottered back against the wall.

"He will kill you!" she heard herself saying to Dimsdale. "He will kill you."

But Dimsdale clung like a limpet. Through the surging uproar of her reeling senses Anne heard his voice.

"Sir Giles! Sir Giles! This won't do, Sir. "You've got a bit beyond yourself. Come along with me, Sir Giles. You are not well. You ought to be in bed. Now, now, Sir Giles! Give it up! Come! Here's West to help you undress."

But Sir Giles fought to be free, cursing hideously, writhing this way and that with Dimsdale hanging on to him; and at sight of the footman hastening to the old man's assistance, he put forth a strength so terrific that he swung him completely off the ground.

"He's too much for me!" shouted Dimsdale. "My Lady, go—go, for the love of heaven! Quick, West! Quick! Trip him! It's the only way! Ah!"

They went down in a fearful, struggling heap,

Sir Giles underneath, but making so violent a fight that the whole room seemed to shake.

And Anne stood and looked upon the whole ghastly spectacle as one turned to stone.

Sir Giles's struggles became less gigantic, became spasmodic, convulsive, futile, and finally ceased altogether. He lay like a dead man, save that his features twitched horribly as if evil spirits were at work upon him.

The whole conflict had occupied but a few minutes, but it had been an eternity of fearful tumult. Yet the hard-breathing silence that followed was almost more terrible still.

Out of it arose old Dimsdale, wiping his forehead with a shaking head.

"He didn't hurt Your Ladyship?" he questioned anxiously.

But she could not take her eyes from the motionless figure upon the floor or answer him.

"My Lady," he said, "come away from here!"

But Anne never stirred.

He laid a very humble hand upon her arm.

"Let me take you downstairs," he urged gently. "There's a friend there waiting for Your Ladyship, a friend as will understand."

"A . . . friend?" She turned her head stiffly, her eyes still striving to remain fixed upon that mighty, inert form.

"Yes, My Lady. He only came a few minutes back. He is waiting in the drawing-room. It was Sir Giles he asked to see, said it was very particular.

It was West here took the message to Sir Giles, and I think it was that as made him come up here so mad like.

"I came after him as soon as I heard. But the gentleman is still waiting, My Lady. Will you see him and—explain?"

"Who is the gentleman?" Anne heard the question, but not as if she herself had uttered it. The voice that spoke seemed to come from an immense distance.

And from equally far seemed to come Dimsdale's answer, though it reached and pierced her understanding in an instant.

"It's Mr. Errol, My Lady, the crippled one. Mr. Lucas, I think his name is."

Anne turned then as sharply as though a voice had called her.

"Lucas Errol! Is he here? Ah, take me to him! Take me to him!"

* * *

The moment Lucas Errol's hand closed upon hers it was to Anne as if an immense and suffocating weight had been lifted from her, and with it all her remaining strength crumbled away as if her burden alone had sustained her.

"Her Ladyship has had a shock, Sir," explained Dimsdale.

"Won't you sit down?" said Lucas gently.

In a moment she found herself sitting on a sofa with Lucas.

"You mustn't mind me, Lady Carfax," he said.

"I know what you have come through. I understand."

Dimly she heard the words, but she could not respond to them. She was shivering, shivering with a violence that she was utterly unable to repress.

Suddenly there came a sound, piercing the silence, a sound that made Anne start upright in wild terror.

"What is it? What is it?"

Instantly and reassuringly Lucas's hand clasped hers.

"Don't be afraid!" he said. "They are moving him to another room, that's all."

She sank back, shuddering, her face hidden. The sound continued, seeming to come nearer, the sound of a man's voice shrieking horribly for help, in piercing accents of terror that might have come from a torture chamber.

Suddenly the yells became articulate, resolved into words: "Anne! Anne! Anne!" in terrible crescendo.

She sprang up with a sharp cry. But on the instant the man beside her spoke.

"Anne, you are not to go."

She paused, irresolute.

"I must! I must! He is calling me!"

"You are not to go," he reiterated, and for the first time she heard the dominant note in his voice. "Come here, child! Come close to me! It will soon be over."

Her irresolution passed like a cloud. She

looked down, saw his blue eyes shining straight up at her, kind still, but compelling. And she dropped upon her knees beside him and hid her face upon his shoulder, with the cry of:

"Help me! Help me! I can't bear it!"

He folded his arms about her as though he were a woman, and held her fast.

A strange peace, wholly unaccountable, fell gently upon her torn spirit. But even then it was long before she moved. She felt an overwhelming reluctance to withdraw herself from the shelter of those quiet arms.

"What must you think of me?" she whispered at last, her face still hidden.

"My dear," he said, "I understand."

He did not offer to release her, but as she moved she found herself free, she found herself able to look into his face.

"I shall never forget your goodness to me," she said very earnestly.

He smiled a little, after a fashion she did not wholly comprehend.

"My dear Lady Carfax, you underrate friendship when you say a thing like that. Sit down, won't you? And let me tell you what brought me here."

"Nap told you . . ." she hazarded.

"Yes, Nap told me. And I decided I had better come at once. I wasn't in when he got back, or I should have been here sooner. I saw there had been a gross misunderstanding, and I hoped I should be able to get your husband to take a reasonable view."

"Ah!" she said, with a shiver. "I . . . I'm thankful you didn't meet."

"I am sorry," Lucas said quietly. And though he said no more, she knew that he was thinking of her.

"How is Nap?" she ventured hesitatingly.

"Nap," he said, with deliberation, "will be himself again in a very few weeks. You need have no anxiety for him."

Again she did not wholly understand his tone. She glanced at him nervously, half-afraid that he was keeping something from her.

"You really mean that?"

His eyes met hers, very level and direct.

"He is badly battered, of course. But he is not quite like other men. He has no nerves to speak of in a physical sense. He will make a quick recovery. Broken bones mean very little to a man of his calibre."

She heard him with an inexpressable relief mingled with wonder.

Chapter Four

The gradual coming of spring that year was like a benediction after the prolonged rigour of the frost. To Anne, it was as though a great peace had descended upon all things, quelling all tumult.

Her husband had been taken to a private Mental Home, where he would receive special treatment. And only once had she been to Baronmead since the masquerade on the ice. It was in fulfilment of her promise to Nap, but she had not seen him.

As the weeks slipped by she began to wonder at his prolonged silence. For no word of any sort reached her from him. He seemed to have forgotten her very existence.

That he was well again she knew from Lucas, who often came over in the motor with his mother.

As his brother had predicted, he had made a rapid recovery; but no sooner was he well than he was gone with a suddenness that surprised no one but Anne.

She was convinced that he would return sooner or later. Whatever appearances might be, she was sure, he had not relinquished the bond of friendship that linked them. Deep in her heart she knew that he would come back.

The news of Sir Giles's illness spread rapidly through the neighbourhood, and people began to be very kind to her.

And Anne tried to be cordial, with the result that on a certain morning in early May there reached her a short friendly note from Mrs. Damer, wife of the M.F.H., begging her to dine with them quite informally on the following night.

"There will only be a few of us, all intimate friends," the note said. "Do come. I have been longing to ask you for such an age."

Anne considered the matter, contemplated an excuse, finally rejected it, and wrote an acceptance.

She wore the dress of shimmering green in which she had appeared at the Hunt Ball. Vividly the memory of that night swept across her. She had not worn it since, and scarcely knew what impulse moved her to don it now.

It well became her stately figure. Dimsdale, awaiting her departure at the hall-door, looked at her with the admiring reverence he might have bestowed upon a Queen.

Again, during her drive through the dark, the memory of that winter night flashed back upon her. She recalled that smooth, noiseless journey in which she had seemed to be borne upon wings.

She recalled her misery and her weariness, her dream and her awakening. Nap had been very good to her that night. He had won her confidence, her gratitude, her friendship.

His reputation notwithstanding, she had trusted him fully, and she had not found him wanting. A faint sigh rose to her lips. She was beginning to miss this friend of hers.

But the next moment she had drawn back sharply and swiftly, as if she had encountered an angel with a flaming sword. This was the path down which she would not wander. Why should she wish to do so? There were so many other paths open to her now.

Entering the drawing-room, she found Major Shirley with his wife and daughter, Ralph and Dot Waring, and the doctor and his wife assembled with their host and hostess.

Mrs. Damer glanced at the clock after greeting them.

"The Errols are late."

Anne chanced to be speaking to Dot at the

moment, and the girl's magic change of countenance called her attention to the words. She wondered if her own face changed, and became uneasily aware of a sudden quickening of the heart.

Dot openly and eagerly watched the door, and Anne with a conscious effort suppressed an inclination to do likewise. When it opened she looked up quite naturally, and no one suspected the wild leaping of her heart.

Nap entered, sleek, trim, complacent; followed by Bertie, whose brown face looked unmistakably sullen.

"Sorry we are late," drawled Nap. "Bertie will make our excuses."

But Bertie said nothing, and it was left to Mrs. Damer to step into the breach. She did so quite gallantly, if somewhat clumsily.

"I am very pleased to see you, Nap, but, you know, it was your brother whom we expected. I didn't so much as know that you were at home."

"Oh, quite so," smiled Nap. "Don't apologise, please!

"So good of you not to mind the exchange. I know I am a poor substitute. But my brother is entertaining an old friend who has arrived unexpectedly, so I persuaded him to send me in his place.

"He charged me with all manner of excuses and apologies, which I will not deliver since I know them to be unnecessary."

Mrs. Damer found it impossible not to smile at his calm effrontery, even though she knew Major Shirley to be frowning behind his back.

"When did you return?" she asked. "Someone said you were in the States."

"I was," said Nap. "I returned half an hour ago; hence our late arrival, for which I humbly beg to apologise."

"Oh, you Americans!" laughed Mrs. Damer. "You are never at a loss. Do let us go in to dinner."

When they went in to dinner Anne discovered that Nap was seated upon her right.

"It's all right," he said coolly. "I was told to sit here, obviously decreed by the gods. You'll think me uncanny if I tell you that it was just this that I came for."

"You are uncanny," she said.

He made her a brief bow. It seemed to her that a mocking spirit gleamed in his eyes. She had never felt less confident of him, less at her ease with him, than at that moment.

She felt as if in some subtle fashion, wholly beyond her comprehension, he were playing some deep-laid game, as if he were weaving some intricate web too secret and too intangible to be understood or grappled with.

Upon one point only was she quite clear. He would suffer no reference to their last meeting. Whatever the effect of that terrible punishment upon him, he did not choose that she should see it.

She had seen him in the utmost extremity of his humiliation, but she should never see the scars that were left.

This much of his attitude she could understand, and understanding could pardon that part which baffled her. But she could not feel at her ease.

"And so you are afraid," said Nap. "That's a new thing for you."

She glanced round the table. In the general hubbub of talk they were as isolated as though they were actually alone together.

"No," she said. "Why should I be afraid? But, I feel as if I am talking to . . . a stranger."

"Perhaps you are," said Nap.

He uttered a laugh she could not fathom, and then with a certain recklessness he said:

"Permit me to present to Your Majesty the Knave of Diamonds!"

There was that in his tone that hurt her, vaguely little as she understood it. She smiled with a hint of wistfulness.

"Surely I have met him before!" she said.

"Without knowing him," said Nap.

"No," she maintained. "I have known him for a long while now. I believe him to be my very good friend."

"What?" he said.

She glanced at him, half-startled by the brief query; but instantly she looked away again with a curious, tingling sense of shock. For it was to her as though she had looked into the heart of a consuming fire.

"Aren't you rather behind the times?" he drawled. "That was, as you say, a long while ago."

The shock passed, leaving her strangely giddy,

as one on the edge of inconceivable depth. She could say no word in answer. She was utterly and hopelessly at a loss.

With scarcely a pause Nap turned to Violet Shirley, who was seated on his right, and plunged without preliminary into a gay flirtation to which all the world was at liberty to listen if it could not approve.

It was with unspeakable relief that Anne rose at length from that dinner-table. She had a deep longing to escape altogether, to go back to the quiet Manor, where at least all was peace.

He had hurt her more subtly than she could have deemed possible. Had his friendship really meant so much to her? Or was it only her pride that suffered to think he valued her so lightly? It seemed that he was fickle then, fickle as everyone declared him to be.

Yet in her heart she did not for a moment believe it. That single glimpse she had had, past the gibing devil in his eyes, deep into the man himself, had told her something different.

He hated her then, he hated her as the cause of his downfall. This seemed the more likely. And yet—and yet—did she really believe this either?

"Dear Lady Carfax, do play to us!" urged her hostess. "It will be such a treat to hear you."

She rose half-mechanically and went to the piano, struck a few chords, and began to play, still so deep in her maze of conjecture that she hardly knew what she had chosen.

"Lady Carfax!"

She started, every nerve suddenly on the alert.

"Don't stop playing!" he said, and as if it were involuntarily she continued to play.

"I am coming to see you tomorrow," he went on. "What time would you like me to call?"

She was silent. But the blood had risen in a great wave to her face and neck. She could feel it racing in every vein.

"Won't you answer me?" he said. "Won't you fix a time?"

There was that in his voice that made her long earnestly to see his face, but she could not. With a great effort she answered:

"I am generally at home in the afternoon."

"Then will you be out to the rest of the world?" he said.

She stilled the wild tumult of her heart with desperate resolution.

"I think you must take your chance of that."

"I am not taking any chances," he said. "I will come at the fashionable hour if you prefer it. But . . ."

He left the sentence unfinished, with a significance that was more imperious than a definite command.

Anne's fingers were trembling over the keys. Sudden uncertainty seized her. She forgot what she was playing, forgot all in the overwhelming desire to see his face. She muffled her confusion in a few soft chords, and turned round.

He was gone.

* * *

All the birds in the Manor Garden were singing on that afternoon in May. The fruit trees were in bloom. The air was full of the indescribable fragrance of bursting flowers. There was no single note of sadness in all the splendid day.

But the woman who paced slowly to and fro under the opening lilacs because she could not rest knew nothing of its sweetness.

The precious peace of the past few weeks had been snatched from her. Restlessly she wandered up and down, up and down. It was a day for dreams, but she was terribly and tragically awake.

When Nap Errol came to her at length with his quick, light tread that was wary and noiseless as a cat's, she knew of his coming long before he reached her, was vividly, painfully aware of him before she turned to look.

Yesterday she had longed to look him in the face, but today she felt she dared not.

Slim and active, he moved across the grass, and there came to her ears a slight jingle of spurs. He had ridden then. A sudden memory of the man's free insolence in the saddle swept over her, his domination, his imperial arrogance.

Turning to meet him, she knew that she was quivering from head to foot. He came straight up to her.

"Have you no welcome for me?" he said.

By sheer physical effort she compelled herself to face him, to meet the fierce, challenging scrutiny which she knew awaited her. She held out her hand to him.

"I am always glad to see you, Nap."

He took her hand in a sinewy, compelling grip.

"Although you prefer good men."

The ground on which she stood seemed to be shaking, yet she forced herself to smile, ignoring his words.

"Let us go and sit down," she suggested.

Close by was a seat under a great lilac tree in full purple bloom. She moved to it and sat down, but Nap remained upon his feet, watching her.

The air was laden with perfume, the wonderful indescribable essence of spring. Throned among the purple flowers above their heads, a thrush was pouring out the rapture that thrilled his tiny life.

The whole world pulsed to the one great melody, the universal, wordless song. Only the man and the woman were silent as intruders in a sacred place.

She looked up very steadily and spoke.

"This seems like holy ground," she said.

Her voice was hushed, yet it had in it a note of pleading. Her eyes besought him.

And in answer Nap leaned down with a sudden, tigerish movement and laid his hand on hers.

"What have I to do with holiness?" he asked. "Anne, come down from that high pedestal of yours! I'm tired of worshipping a goddess. I want a woman—a woman! I shall worship you none the less because I hold you in my arms."

For a long second she sat quite still, almost as if stunned. Then sharply she turned her face aside, as one turns from the unbearable heat and radiance when the door of a blast-furnace is suddenly opened.

"Oh, Nap," she said, and there was a sound of heartbreak in her words. "What a pity!"

"Why?" he demanded fiercely. "I have the right to speak, to claim my own. Are you going to deny it—you who always speak the truth?"

"You have no right," she answered, still with her face averted. "No man has ever the faintest right to say to another man's wife what you have just said to me."

"And you think I will give you up," he said, "for that?"

She did not at once reply. Only after a moment she freed her hands from his hold, and the action seemed to give her strength. She spoke, her voice very clear and resolute.

"I am not going to say anything unkind to you. You have already borne too much for my sake. But . . . you must know that this is the end of everything. It is the dividing of the ways . . . where we must say good-bye."

"Is it?" he said. He looked down at her with his brief, thin-lipped smile. "Then, if that's so, look at me—look at me, Anne, and tell me that you don't love me."

She made an almost convulsive gesture of protest and sat silent.

"That being so," he said very deliberately, "there is no power on earth, I swear—I swear—that shall ultimately come between us."

"Hush!" She turned towards him, her face

white and agitated. "I will not listen to you, Nap. I cannot listen to you. You must go."

She stretched a hand towards him appealingly, and he caught it, crushing it against his breast. For a moment he seemed about to kneel, and then he altered his purpose and drew her to her feet.

Again she was aware of that subtle, mysterious force within him, battling with her, seeking to dominate, to conquer, to overwhelm her. She seemed to totter on the very edge of the pit of destruction.

Very quietly at length his voice came to her. It held just a touch of ridicule.

"What! Still doing sacrifice to the great god Convention! My dear girl, but you are preposterous! Do you seriously believe that I will suffer that drunken maniac to come between us—now?"

He flung his head back with the words. His fiery eyes seemed to scorch her. And overhead a rapturous bird-voice pealed forth a perfect paean of victory.

But Anne stood rigid, unresponsive as an image of stone.

"He is my husband."

She felt his hand tighten upon hers, till the pressure was almost more than she could endure.

"You never felt a spark of love for him!" he said. "You married him—curse him!—against your will!"

"Nevertheless, I married him," she said.

He showed his teeth for a moment, and was

silent. Then imperiously he swept up his forces for the charge.

"These things are provided for in the States," he said. "If you won't come to me without the sanction of the law, I will wait while you get it. I will wait till you are free, till I can make you my lawful wife. That's a fair offer anyway."

He began to smile.

"See what a slave you have made of me!" he said. "I've never offered any woman marriage before."

But Anne broke in upon him almost fiercely.

"Oh, don't you know me better than that?" she said. "Nap, I am not the sort of woman to throw off the yoke like that. It is true that I never loved him, and I do not think that I shall ever live with him again. But still . . . I married him, and while he lives I shall never be free . . . never, never!"

"Yet you are mine," he said.

"No . . . no!"

She sought to free her hand, but he kept it.

"Look at me!" he said. "Do you remember that day in March, the day you saw me whipped like a dog!"

Involuntarily she raised her eyes to his.

"Oh, don't," she whispered, shuddering. "Don't!"

But he persisted.

"You felt that thrashing far more than I did, though it made a murderer of me. You were furious for my sake. Did you never ask yourself why?"

Then in a lower voice, bending towards her:

"Do you think I didn't know the moment I saw your face above mine? Do you think I didn't feel the love in your arms, holding me up? Do you think it isn't in your eyes, even now?"

"Oh, hush!" she said again piteously. "Nap, you are hurting me. I cannot bear it. Even if it were so, love . . . true love . . . is a sacred thing . . . not to be turned into sin."

"Sin!" he said. "What is sin? Is it sin to fulfil the very purpose for which you were created?"

But at that she winced so sharply that he knew he had gone too far. It was characteristic of the man that he made no attempt to recover lost ground.

"I'm a wicked pagan, no doubt," he said, with a touch of recklessness. "Everyone will tell you so. I fancy I've told you so myself more than once. Yet you needn't shrink as if I were unclean. I have done nothing that you would hate me for since I have known you."

He paused and seemed to listen, then very quietly released her hand. A curious expression flickered across his face as he did so, and a little chill went through her. It was like the closing of the furnace door.

"I am going," he said. "But I shall come back —I shall come back."

His smile, sudden and magnetic, gleamed for an instant and was gone. "Do you remember the missing heart?" he asked. "There are some things that I never forget."

And so, without farewell, he turned and left her, moving swiftly and easily over the grass. She heard the jingle of his spurs but no sound of any footfall as he went.

* * *

"My Lady!"

Anne looked up with a start. She had been sitting with closed eyes under the lilac tree.

Dimsdale, discreet and deferential as ever, stood before her.

"Mr. Lucas Errol is here," he told her, "with another gentleman. I knew Your Ladyship would wish to be at home to him."

"Oh, certainly," she answered, rising. "I am always at home to Mr. Lucas Errol. Please tell him I am coming immediately."

With the quiet dignity peculiar to her, she passed up the garden path.

She found her visitors in the drawing-room, which she entered by the open window. Lucas greeted her with his quiet smile and introduced Capper—"a very great friend of mine, and incidentally the finest Doctor in the U.S.A."

As she sat at the tea-table and dispensed hospitality to her guests it was Lucas who kept the conversation going. She thought he seemed in wonderful spirits.

Capper sat in almost unbroken silence. Quite suddenly at length he set down his cup.

"Lady Carfax," he said abruptly. "I'm told you have a herb garden. Will you take me to see it while Lucas enjoys a much-needed rest?"

Anne glanced up in surprise. They were almost the first words he had spoken. Capper was already upon his feet.

"Of course, I will do so with pleasure," Anne replied, and turned to the window. They went out together into the golden spring evening.

They were out of sight of the house before he spoke.

"Say, Madam, I'm told you know the Errol family well."

She glanced at him in surprise.

"Of course I know them all."

"You're real friendly. With which one in particular?"

She hesitated momentarily.

"I am very fond of Mrs. Errol," she said, speaking very quietly. "But Nap was my first friend, and afterwards Lucas. . . ."

"Oh, Nap!"

There was such withering contempt in the exclamation that she had perforce to remark upon it.

"Nap is evidently no favourite with you," she said.

He raised his brows till they nearly met his hair.

"Nap, my dear lady," he drily observed, "is doubtless all right in his own sphere. It isn't mine. I came over to this country at his request and in his company, and a queerer devil it has never been my lot to encounter.

"But what can you expect? I've never yet seen him in a blanket and moccasins, but I imagine that he'd be considerably preferable that way. I guess he's just a fish out of water on this side of civilisation."

"What can you mean?" Anne said.

For the second time that afternoon she felt as if the ground beneath her had begun to tremble. She looked up at him with troubled eyes. Surely the whole world was rocking!

"I mean what I say, Madam," he told her curtly. "There is a powerful streak of red in Nap Errol's blood, or I am much mistaken."

"Ah!" Anne exclaimed.

"I don't say the fellow is an out-and-out savage," Capper went on. "P'r'aps he'd be more tolerable if he were. But the fatal streak is there. Never noticed it? I thought you women noticed everything. Talk of the devil in New York and you very soon find the conversation drifting round to Nap Errol."

He paused and then continued.

"Now and then he has a lapse into sheer savagery, and then there is no controlling him. It's just as the fit takes him. He's never to be trusted. It's an ineradicable taint."

She shivered at the words, but still she did not speak. Capper went unconcernedly on.

"I fancy Lucas once thought he was going to make a gentleman of him. Teach a tiger to sit up and beg! He has a most amazing patience, but I guess even he realizes by now that the beast is untamable. Mrs. Errol saw it long ago. You know Mrs. Errol, you say?"

"Yes, I know her." Anne heard the words but was not conscious of uttering them.

Capper gave her a single straight look.

"You wouldn't think, would you," said he, "that that woman carries a broken heart about with her? But I assure you that's so. Nap Errol was the tragedy of her life."

That quickened her to interest. She was conscious of a gradual sinking downwards of her dismay till it came to rest somewhere deep in her inmost soul, leaving the surface free for other impressions.

"He came out of nowhere," Capper went on. "She never tried to account for him. He was her husband's son. She made him hers. But he's been a tiger's cub all his life, a hurricane, a firebrand. He and Bertie are usually at daggers drawn and Lucas spends his time keeping the peace—which is about as wearing an occupation for a sick man as I can imagine."

His voice was hard as he said:

"I want to put a stop to it, Lady Carfax. I speak as one family friend to another. Lucas seems to like you. I believe you could make him see reason if you took the trouble."

"Will you tell me," Anne said, "what it is that you want to do?"

Capper shot her a keen side-glance.

"I want to cure him," he said. "I want to make a whole man of him."

"Could you?" she asked.

"I could." Abruptly Capper stopped. "If I

could choose my conditions. If I could banish that pestilent brother of his, if I could rouse him to something like energy. Given his whole-hearted co-operation, I could do it."

"It would mean an operation then. A very serious one?" Anne paused upon the green path. Her eyes sought Capper's.

"My dear lady, it would mean not one, but two," he answered her with curt directness. "I won't trouble you with technical details, but both operations would be a serious tax upon his strength, and freedom from all anxiety is essential. That fellow Nap is the principal obstacle."

"If you consider Nap an obstacle, why don't you speak to him?" Anne asked in her quiet voice.

Capper shrugged his shoulders.

"He hates me, and small wonder! I've told him the brutal truth too often."

"And Lucas does not wish to undergo the operation?"

"That's just the infernal part of it!" burst forth Capper. "He would undergo it tomorrow if he didn't consider himself indispensable to his brother.

"And, Lady Carfax, he wants help. He wants someone strong to stand by. I believe you could do it, if you would. You are the sort of woman that men turn to in trouble. I've been watching you. I know."

Again very faintly Anne smiled, with more patience than amusement.

"Dr. Capper, has Lucas been telling you about me?"

"Yes."

"You know how I am situated?" she questioned.

"I do."

"And you think I could be of use to him?"

"I know you could. I'll tell you something, I love Lucas Errol as if he were my son."

"I think we all love him in our different ways," Anne said gently.

"That so?" said the American keenly. "Then I shall leave the matter in your charge, Lady Carfax. I can see you're a capable woman.

"I'm coming back in September to perform that operation. You will have a willing patient ready for me, and my bugbear, Nap—that most lurid specimen of civilised devilry—hunting scalps on the other side of the Atlantic."

"Oh, I don't know!" Anne said quickly. "But I will do my best." She spoke breathlessly, as one suddenly plunged into a strong current.

"Then I'm not afraid," said Capper. "We shall pull him through between us. It will be a miracle, of course, but"—a sudden smile flashed across his face, transforming him completely—"miracles happen, Lady Carfax."

* * *

Slowly Anne drew aside the curtain and looked forth into the night, a magic night, soft and wonderful, infinitely peaceful.

With no effort of hers the events of that afternoon passed before her. She heard again the ardent voice of the friend who had become the lover. He had loved her from the first, it seemed, and she had not known it. Could it be that she had loved him also, all unknowing?

There came again to her the memory of those fierce, compelling eyes, the dogged mastery with which he had fought her resolution, the sudden magic softening of the harsh face when he smiled.

There came again the passionate thrilling of his voice; again her hands tingled in that close grip; again she thought she felt the beating of the savage heart.

She raised her arms above her head with the gesture of one who wards off something immense, but they fell almost immediately. She was so tired . . . so tired. She had fought so hard and so long.

Oh, why was there no peace for her? What had she done to be thus tortured? Why had love come to her at all? In all her barren life she had never asked for love.

What had she to do with love . . . love, moreover, for a man who could offer her but the fiery passion of a savage, a man from whom her every instinct shrank, who mocked at holy things and overthrew all barriers of convention with a cynicism that silenced all protest.

The quiet garden lay sleeping before her in the moonlight, and she felt as if God must be very far away. She was very terribly alone that night.

The impulse came to her to pass out into the dewy stillness, and she obeyed it, scarcely knowing what she did. Over the silver grass, ghost-like, she moved. It was as if a voice had called her.

On to the lilac trees with their burden of fragrant blossoms, where the thrush had raised his song of rapture, where she had faced that first fiery ordeal of love.

She reached the bench where she had sat that afternoon. The midnight peace lay like a shroud upon all things. But suddenly fear stabbed her, piercing every nerve to quivering activity. She knew . . . how, she could not have said . . . that she was no longer alone.

She stood quite still, but the beating of her heart rose quick and insistent in her ears, like the beat of a drum. Swift came the conviction that it was no inner impulse that had brought her hither. She had obeyed a voice that called.

For many seconds she stood motionless, not breathing, not daring to turn her head. Then, as her strength partially returned, she took two steps forward to the seat under the lilac tree, and, her hand upon the back of it, she spoke.

"Nap!"

He came, gliding like a shadow behind her. Slowly she turned and faced him.

He was still in riding-dress. She heard again the faint jingle of his spurs. Yet the moonlight shone strangely down upon him, revealing in him something foreign, something incongruous, that she marvelled that she had never before noticed.

The fierce, dusky face with its glittering eyes and savage mouth was oddly unfamiliar to her, though she knew it all by heart. In imagination she clothed him with the blanket and moccasins of Capper's uncouth speech; and she was afraid.

She did not know how to break the silence. The heart within her was leaping like a wild thing in captivity.

"Why are you here?" she said at last, and she knew that her voice shook.

He answered her instantly, with a certain doggedness.

"I want to know what Capper has been saying to you."

She started almost guiltily. Her nerves were on edge that night.

"You may as well tell me," he said coolly. "Sooner or later I am bound to know."

"Then it must be later," she said. "I cannot stay to talk with you now."

"Why not?" he said.

Desperately she faced him, for her heart still quaked within her. The shock of Capper's revelation was still upon her. He had come to her too soon.

"Nap," she said, "I ask you to leave me, and I mean it. Please go!"

But he only drew nearer to her, and she saw that his face was stern. He thrust it forward and regarded her closely.

"So," he said slowly, "he has told you all about me, has he?"

She bent her head. It was useless to attempt to evade the matter now.

"I am mightily obliged to him," said Nap. "I wanted you to know."

Anne was silent.

"I meant to have told you myself. I even began to tell you once, but somehow you put me off. It was that night at Baronmead, you remember?—the night you wanted to help me."

Well she remembered that night, the man's scarcely veiled despair, his bitter railing against the ironies of life. So this had been the meaning of it all. A thrill of pity went through her.

"Yes," he said. "I knew you'd be sorry for me. I guess pity is about the cheapest commodity on the market. But, you'll hardly believe it, I don't want your pity. After all, a man is himself, and it can't be of much importance where he springs from—anyway, to the woman who loves him."

He spoke recklessly, and yet she seemed to detect a vein of entreaty in his words. She steeled her heart against it, but it affected her none the less.

"Nap," she said firmly, "there must be no more talk of love between us. I told you this afternoon that I would not listen, and I will not. Do you understand me? It must end here and now. I am in earnest."

"You don't say!" said Nap.

He was standing close to her, and again fear stabbed her.

"I am in earnest," she said again. But she could not meet his eyes any longer. She dared not let him read her soul just then.

"I am in earnest, too," said Nap. "But you

needn't be afraid of me on that account. I may be a savage, but I'm not despicable. If I take more than you are prepared to offer it's only because I know it to be my own."

He bent towards her, trying to see her face.

"My own, Anne!" he said again very softly. "My own!"

But at his movement she drew back sharply, with a gesture of such instinctive, such involuntary, recoil that in an instant she knew that she had betrayed that which she had sought to hide.

He stiffened as if at a blow, and she saw his hands clench.

In the silence that followed she stood waiting for the storm to burst, waiting for his savagery to tear asunder all restraining bonds and leap forth in devilish fury. But, by what means she knew not, he held it back.

"So," he said at last, his voice very low, "the Queen has no further use for her jester!"

Her heart smote her. What had she done? She felt as if she had cruelly wounded a friend. But because he demanded of her more than friendship she dared not attempt to allay the hurt. She stood silent.

"Can't you find another *role* for me?" he said. "You will find it difficult to exclude me altogether from the cast."

Something in his tone pierced her, compelled her. She glanced up swiftly, met his eyes, and was suddenly caught, as it were, in fiery chains, so that she could not look away.

And there before her the gates of hell opened, and she saw a man's soul in torment. She saw the flames mount higher and higher, scorching and shrivelling and destroying, till at last she could bear the sight no longer. She covered her face with her hands.

"Oh, Nap," she moaned, "if you love me . . . if you love me . . ."

"If I love you . . ." he said.

He put his hand on her shoulder and she trembled from head to foot.

"Prove your love!" she whispered, her face still hidden.

He stood awhile motionless, still with his hand upon her. But at last it fell away.

"You doubt my love then?" he said, and his voice sounded strange to her, almost cold. "You think my love is unworthy of you? You have—lost faith in me?"

She was silent.

"Is it so?" he persisted. "Tell me the truth. I may as well know it. You think, because I am not what Capper would term a thoroughbred, that I am incapable of love. Isn't that so?"

But still she did not answer him. Only, being free, she turned to the garden-seat and sank down upon it, her arms stretched along the back, her head bowed low.

He began to pace up and down like a caged animal, pausing each time he passed her, and each time moving on again as if invisibly urged. At last very suddenly he stopped with his back to her, and stood like a statue in the moonlight.

She did not look at him. She was too near the end of her strength. Her heart was beating very slowly, like a run-down watch. She felt like an old, old woman, utterly tired of life. And she was cold, cold from head to foot.

Minutes passed. Somewhere away in the night an owl hooted, and Nap turned his head sharply, as one accustomed to taking note of every sound.

Awhile longer he stood, seeming to listen, every limb alert and tense, then swiftly he wheeled and gazed full at the drooping woman's figure on the bench.

Slowly his attitude changed. Something that was bestial went out of it; something that was human took its place. Quietly at length he crossed the moonlit space that intervened between them, reached her, knelt beside her.

"Anne," he said, and all her life she remembered the deep melancholy of his voice, "I am a savage, a brute, a devil. But I swear that I have it in me to love you, as you deserve to be loved."

He paused.

"Won't you have patience with me? Won't you give me a chance, the only chance I've ever had, of getting above myself, of learning what love can be? Won't you trust me with your friendship once more? Believe me, I'm not all brute."

She thrilled like a dead thing waked to life.

Her dread of the man passed away like an evil dream, such was the magic he had for her. She slipped one of her cold hands down to him. He caught it, bowed his head upon it, pressed it against his eyes, then lifted his face and looked up at her.

"It is not the end then? You haven't given me up in disgust?"

And she answered him in the only way possible to her.

"I will be your friend still, only . . . only let there never again be any talk of love between us. That alone will end our friendship. Can I trust you? Nap, can I?"

He jerked back his head at the question, and showed her his face in the full moonlight. And she saw that his eyes were still and passionless, unfathomable as a mountain pool.

"If you can bring yourself—if you will stoop—to kiss me," he said, "I think you will know."

She started at the words, but his voice was as steady as his eyes. He asked this thing of her as a sign of her forgiveness, of her friendship, of her trust; and every generous impulse urged her to grant it.

She leaned towards him; she laid her hands upon his shoulders.

"In token of my trust!" she said, and bent to kiss his forehead.

But he gave her his lips instead, the thin, cynical lips that were wont to smile so bitterly. There was no bitterness about them now.

Then he rose in unbroken silence, and went away.

* * *

During the weeks that followed, something of her former tranquility came back to Anne. It was evident that Nap was determined to show himself worthy of her trust, for never by word or look did he make the slightest reference to what had passed between them.

He came and went after his customary sudden fashion. But his absences were never of long duration, and Anne met him fairly frequently.

Her happiest hours were those she spent with Lucas and his mother in the great music-room at Baronmead. It was here also that she learned to know of that hidden, vital quantity, elusive as flame, that was Nap Errol's soul.

For here he would often join them, and the music he drew from his violin, weirdly passionate, with a pathos no words could ever utter, was to Anne the very expression of the man's complex being.

There were times when she could hardly hear that wild music of his without tears. It was like the crying of something that was lost.

Nap would play on and on in the quiet room, as though he played for her alone, with the sure hand of a master upon the quivering strings of his woman's heart.

If Anne was at peace with Nap, Dot was not. She was always on edge when he appeared.

"Can't you and Nap be friends?" Anne asked.

She was becoming increasingly conscious of the tension which emanated from Dot whenever Nap was present.

"No," Dot murmured. "I hate him!"

It was at this moment that Nap walked in. Even Anne was for the moment disconcerted by the abruptness of his entrance, while Dot sprang to her feet with burning cheeks.

In the pause that ensued, Anne rose and put her arm reassuringly through Dot's.

Nap glanced at her.

"That's rather shabby of you," he declared. "I was just going to ask for your support myself."

She smiled at him faintly.

"I think you can manage without it. Dot will not refuse her forgiveness if you ask for it properly."

"Won't she?" Nap said, still keenly watching the girl's half-averted face. "I should if I were Dot. You see, our feud is of very long standing. But I have forgotten what the primary reason was."

"I . . . haven't," said Dot, in a very low voice. Her lower lip was quivering. She bit it desperately.

"What was it?" he asked.

"You . . . told someone . . . I heard you . . . that I was running after Bertie for his . . . money."

"Great Christopher!" said Nap. "You don't say you took that seriously?"

"Of course I did," she said, on the verge of tears.

"Ye gods!" said Nap. "And I've been wondering why on earth you and Bertie couldn't make up your minds! So I've been the obstacle, have I? "We'll put this right at once. Where's Bertie?"

"Oh, no!" Dot said nervously. "No! Don't call him! He'll see I've been crying. Nap . . . please!"

She disengaged herself from Anne, and sprang after him, seizing him impetuously by the arm.

"I mean . . . Mr. Errol!" she substituted in confusion.

He clapped his hand upon hers.

"You can call me anything under the sun that occurs to you as suitable," he said.

"I don't deal in excuses, but when I tell you that I was rather badly up against something at the time, p'r'aps you'll be magnanimous enough to forgive me. Will you?"

"Of course I will!" she said impulsively. "Let's be friends, shall we?"

He gripped her hand.

"Suppose we go and get some tea," he said. "Are you coming, Lady Carfax?"

"I'm not fit to be seen," objected Dot, hanging back.

He drew her on, her hand still fast in his.

"Don't be shy, my dear girl! You look all right. Will you lead the way, Lady Carfax?"

Very reluctantly Dot submitted.

The hall was full of people to whom Mrs. Errol was dispensing tea, assisted by Bertie, when Anne entered, closely followed by Dot and Nap.

Bertie looked at them, then finally stood up and set down his cup abruptly. Nap came towards him, still holding Dot by the hand.

"Hullo, Bertie!" he said, and smote him on the shoulder with a vigorous hand. "I've just been hearing about your engagement, my dear fellow. Congratulations! May you and Dot have the best of everything all your lives!"

Poor Dot would have fled had that been possible, but Nap had transferred her hand to Bertie's, and the boy's warm grasp renewed her fainting courage. She knew he was as amazed as she was herself at Nap's sudden move.

People crowded round them with kindly words, shook hands, chaffed them both, and seemed to be genuinely pleased with the turn of events.

Across the noise and confusion Anne met Nap's eyes and smiled. He had made Dot and Bertie happy and she felt a sudden warmth for him which she could not deny.

* * *

Anne found herself the first to enter the drawing-room that night before dinner. She was staying the night, but planned to return home the following day.

A groom had brought her letters from home, and she sat down to peruse them by an open window.

The evening sun poured full upon her in fiery splendour, and she opened the first letter mechanically. Her thoughts were wandering. Then she saw that it was from a Doctor in the Mental Home. Slowly her eyes travelled along the page.

When she turned it at length her hands were shaking so much that the paper rattled and quivered like a living thing. The writing ended on the further page, but before her eyes reached the signature, the letter had fallen from her grasp.

Anne, the calm, the self-contained, the stately, sat huddled in her chair—a trembling, stricken woman, with her hands pressed tightly over her eyes, as if to shut out some dread vision.

In the silence that followed, someone entered the room with a light, cat-like tread and approached the window against which she sat.

So overwhelmed was she for the moment that she was unaware of any presence till Nap's voice spoke to her, and she started to find him close to her, within reach of her hand.

She lifted her white face then, while mechanically she groped for the letter. It had fallen to the ground. He picked it up.

"What is it?" he asked, and she thought his voice sounded harsh. "You have had bad news?"

She held out her hand for the letter.

"No, it is good. I . . . am a little tired, that's all."

"That is not all," he said, and she heard the dogged note in his voice that she had come to know as the signal of indomitable resolution.

He sat down on the window-seat close to her, still keeping the letter in his hand.

She made a little hopeless gesture and sat silent, striving for composure. She knew that during the seconds that followed, his eyes never stirred from her face.

She turned her head at last and spoke.

"You may read that letter," she said.

"I have read it already."

She started slightly, meeting his eyes.

"In your face," he told her. "It contains news of the man you call your husband. It is to say he is better—and—coming—home."

He spoke the last words as though he were actually reading them one by one in her tragic eyes.

"It is an experiment," she whispered. "He wishes it himself, it seems, and they think the change might prove beneficial. He is decidedly better, marvellously so. And he has expressed a desire to see me."

She faltered but continued.

"I should not be . . . alone with him. There will be an attendant. But . . . but you mustn't think I am afraid. It wasn't that. Only . . . only . . . I did not expect it. It has come rather suddenly. I am not so easily upset as a rule."

She spoke hurriedly, almost as if she were pleading with him to understand and to pardon her weakness.

But her words quivered into silence. Nap said nothing whatever. He sat motionless, the letter still in his hand, his eyes unswervingly fixed upon her.

That sphinx-like stare became unbearable at last. She gathered her strength and rose.

"You came upon me at an unlucky . . . moment," she said. "Please . . . forget it."

He still stared at her stonily without moving or

speaking. Something that was almost fear gripped her. The very stillness of the man was in a fashion intimidating.

An instant later, while she still waited for him to speak, he turned on his heel and left her.

Anne covered a deep uneasiness beneath her resolute serenity of manner. She could not forget that basilisk stare. It haunted her almost to the exclusion of everything else.

She had no thought to spare for the letter regarding her husband. She could only think of Nap. What had that stare concealed? She felt that if she could have got past those baffling, challenging eyes she would have seen something terrible.

Yet when she met him again she wondered if after all she had disquieted herself for naught. He did not speak to her, did not, she fancied, even look at her; but after a few dumb seconds his hand came out to hers and held it in a close, sinewy grip. Her own was nerveless, cold as ice.

She could not have withdrawn it had she wished. But she did not wish. That action of his had a strange effect upon her, subtly calming her reawakened doubts. She felt that he meant to reassure her, and she suffered herself to be reassured.

Later, she marvelled at the ingenuity that had so successfully blinded her, marvelled at herself for having been so blinded, marvelled most of all at the self-restraint that could so shackle and smother the fierce passion that ran like liquid fire in every vein as to make her fancy that it had ceased to be.

Only to Lucas could she speak of what had happened.

"Mr. Errol, I have had news of . . . my husband. He wants to come home. No, he is not well yet, but decidedly better, well enough to be at liberty in the charge of an attendant. And so . . . and so . . ."

Words failed. She became silent, waiting for the steady sympathy which she knew she would receive.

But Lucas did not speak at once. It almost seemed as if he were at a loss. It almost seemed as if he realized too fully for speech that leaden weight of despair which had for a space so terribly overwhelmed her.

And then at last his voice came to her, slow and gentle, yet with a vital note in it that was like a bugle-call to her tired spirit.

"Stick to it, Lady Carfax! You'll win out. You're through the worst already."

Desperately, as one half-ashamed, she answered him.

"I wish with all my heart I could think so. But I am still asking myself if . . . if there is no way of escape."

"Thank you for telling me," he said very simply. "But you'll win out all the same. I have always known that you were on the winning side."

The words touched her in a fashion not wholly accountable. Her eyes filled with sudden tears.

"What makes you have such faith in me?" she said.

"That's just one of the things I can't explain," he said. "But I think God made you for a spar for drowning men to cling to."

She smiled with him in spite of her tears.

"May the spar never fail."

"I am not afraid," he answered very steadily.

* * *

Anne slept and dreamed, a wild and fearful dream.

She dreamed that she was on horseback, galloping, galloping, galloping, in headlong flight from someone of whom she was unspeakably afraid. And ever behind her at break-neck speed, gaining upon her, merciless as fate, galloped her pursuer.

It was terrible, it was agonising, yet, though in her heart she knew it to be a dream, she could not wake. And then, all suddenly, the race was over. Someone drew abreast of her.

A sinewy hand gripped her bridle-rein. With a gasping cry she turned to face her captor, and saw . . . a Red Indian! His tigerish eyes gazed into hers.

He was laughing with a fiendish exultation. The eagle-feathers tossed above his swarthy face. It came nearer to her; it glared into her own. And suddenly recognition stabbed her like a sword. It was the face of Nap Errol. . . .

He was on the stairs talking to Hudson, the valet, when she descended to breakfast, but he turned at once to greet her.

"I am sorry to say Lucas has had a bad night.

He will keep to his room today. How have you slept, Lady Carfax?"

She answered him conventionally. They went downstairs together.

Bertie was in the hall, studying a newspaper. He came forward, scowling heavily, shook hands with Anne, and immediately addressed his brother.

"I've just come in from the stables. Have you been out all night? You've nearly ridden the mare to death."

Anne glanced at Nap instinctively. He was smiling.

"Don't vex yourself, my good Bertie," he said. "The mare will be all right after a feed."

"Will she?" growled Bertie. "She is half-dead from exhaustion anyway."

"Oh, skittles!" said Nap, turning to go.

The boy's indignation leaped to a glaze.

"Skittles to you! I know what I'm saying. And if you're not ashamed of yourself, you damned well ought to be!"

Nap stopped.

"What?" he drawled.

Bertie glared at him and subsided. The explosion had been somewhat more violent than he had intended.

Very quietly Nap stepped up to him.

"Will you repeat that last remark of yours?"

Bertie was silent.

"Or do you prefer to withdraw it?"

Bertie maintained a dogged silence. He was

fidgeting with the paper in a fashion that seemed to indicate embarrassment.

"Do you withdraw it?" Nap repeated, still quiet, still slightly drawling.

Bertie hunched his shoulders like a schoolboy.

"Oh, get away, Nap!" he growled. "Yes, sorry I spoke. Now clear out and leave me alone!"

Anne was already at the further end of the hall, but Nap overtook her before she entered the breakfast-room. He opened the door for her, and as she passed him she saw that he was faintly smiling.

"Pardon the contretemps!" he said. "You may have noticed before that I am not particularly good at swallowing insults."

"I wonder if there was a cause for it," she said, looking at him steadily. "Remember, I know what your riding is like."

He raised his eyebrows for a moment, then laughed.

He attended to her wants and his own, and finally sat down facing her. He seemed to be in excellent spirits.

"Please, don't be so severe!" he urged. "Just as I am going to ask a favour of you, too!"

She smiled a little but not very willingly.

"I don't like cruel people," she said. "Cruelty is a thing I can never forget, because I abhor it so."

"And are you never cruel?" said Nap.

"I hope not."

"I hope not too," he rejoined, giving her a hard look. "But I sometimes have my doubts."

He smiled at her.

"Queen Anne, I crave a boon."

Almost involuntarily she returned his smile. "So you said before."

"And you don't even ask what it is."

"I am not quite sure that I want to know, Nap," she said.

"You are not liking me this morning," he observed.

She made no answer.

"What is it?" he said. "Is it the mare?"

"Perhaps, in part."

"And the other part?" He leaned forward, looking at her keenly. "Are you afraid of me, Anne?"

His voice was free from reproach, yet her heart smote her. She reminded herself of how he had once pleaded with her for her trust.

"I'm sorry I pressed the mare," he said. "But Bertie exaggerated. I will fetch him in and make him own it if you like."

"No, don't, please! I think Bertie was probably in the right."

"Do you, though?" Nap leaned back again, regarding her with supercilious attention. "It's rather—daring of you to say so."

"Do you really think I stand in awe of you?" she said.

"You are such a truly remarkable woman," he

made answer, "that I scarcely know what to think. But since you are not afraid of me, apparently, perhaps I may venture to come to the point. Do you know I have been laying plans for a surprise picnic for you and—one other? It's such a gorgeous day. Don't refuse!"

The boyish note she liked to hear sounded suddenly in his voice. He discarded his cynicism and leaned towards her again, eager, persuasive.

"Don't refuse," he reiterated. "Look at the sunshine, listen to the birds, think of a whole day in the open! I'll take you to the loveliest place I know on this quaint little island. Don't look prudish. Be a girl for once. Never mind the rest of creation. No one else will know anything about it."

His voice was irresistible as he pleaded.

"We leave Baronmead this morning in the motor, and who cares what time we reach the Manor? It can't matter to you or anyone. Say you'll come! Say it!"

"My dear Nap!" Anne looked at him dubiously, uncertain whether to take him seriously.

"Say it!" he repeated. "There is no earthly reason why you shouldn't. And I'll take such care of you. Why shouldn't you have a good time for once? You never have had in all your life."

True, only too true! But it was not that fact that made her waver.

"Will you tell me what plans you have made for this picnic?" she asked at length.

He began to smile.

"My plans, Lady Carfax, are entirely subject

to your approval. About forty miles from here there is a place called Bramhurst, a place after your own heart, a paradise. With judicious driving we could be there by one or soon after, in time for luncheon."

"Yes?" she said, as he stopped.

"That's all," said Nap.

"But . . . afterwards?" she hazarded.

"My dear Lady Carfax, if it is to be a surprise picnic, where's the use of settling all the details beforehand?"

Nap's tone was one of indulgent protest; he was eating and drinking rapidly, as if he had an appointment to keep.

"My suggestion is that we then follow our inclinations—your inclinations." He smiled at her again. "I am your slave till sunset."

"Could we be back at the Manor by then?" she asked.

"Of course we could."

"Will you promise that we shall be?" She looked up at him seriously.

He was still smiling.

"If you ordain it."

"I must be back by dinner-time."

"And you dine . . . ?"

"At eight."

He pushed back his chair and rose.

"Very discreet of you! The sun sets at eight-ten. At what hour will you deign to be ready?"

"At eleven," said Anne.

He glanced at his watch.

"I am afraid you can't see Lucas to say good-bye. Hudson has just given him morphia."

"Is he so bad then?" she asked quickly.

"No worse than he has been before. Bad pain all night. He always fights against taking the stuff. I persuaded him."

He spoke shortly, as if the subject were distasteful to him.

"No doubt he is easier by this time. Eleven o'clock then! I will go and get ready."

Then he paused, his hand on the back of her chair.

"Can you keep a secret?" he asked lightly.

She glanced up at him.

"A secret?"

"Let this be a secret between yourself and your humble slave!"

And with the words he turned with an air of finality and went away.

* * *

Nap drove in almost unbroken silence. Anne had no clue to his thoughts; but she scarcely speculated about him. She did not want to talk.

She only desired to give herself up to the pure pleasure of rapid movement. She had complete faith in his driving. If daring, he was never reckless with her beside him.

Only when they emerged at last upon a wide moor, where the early heather grew in tufts of deepest rose, she cried to him suddenly to stop.

"I must get some of it. It is the first I have seen. Look! How exquisite!"

He drew up at the side of the long white road that zigzagged over the moor, and they went together into the springy heath, wading in it after the waxen flowers.

Anne sat down in the blazing sunshine and lifted her clear eyes to his.

"I won't thank you, because we are friends," she said. "But this is the best day I have ever had."

He sat down beside her.

"So you are not sorry you came?"

"I could not be sorry today," she answered. "How long have you known this perfect place?"

He lay back in the heather with his arms flung wide.

"I came here first one day in the spring, a day in May. The place was a blaze of gorse and broom, as if it were on fire. It suited me, for I was on fire too."

In the silence that succeeded his words he turned and leisurely scrutinised her. She was snapping a stalk of heather with minute care. A deep flush rose and spread over her face under his eyes.

"Why don't you look at me?" he asked.

Very slowly her eyes came down to him. He was smiling in a secret fashion, not as if he expected her to smile in return. The sunlight beat down upon his upturned face. He blinked at her lazily and stretched every limb in succession, like a cat.

"Let me know when you begin to feel bored," he said. "I am quite ready to amuse you."

"I thought it was only the bores who were ever bored," she said.

He opened his eyes a little.

"Did I say that or did you?"

"I believe you said it originally."

"I remember," he returned composedly. "It was on the night you bestowed upon me the office of Court jester, the night you dreamed I was the Knave of Diamonds, the night that . . ."

She interrupted very gently but very resolutely:

"The night that we became friends, Nap."

"A good many things happened that night," he remarked. "Have you ever dreamed about me since that night?"

She was silent, all her attention concentrated upon her bunch of heather. His eyes left her face and began to study her hands.

After a moment he pulled a bit of string out of his pocket and without a word proceeded to wind it round the stalks she held. As he knotted it he spoke.

"So that is why you were afraid of me today. I knew there was something. Whenever I hold your hand in mine I can see into your soul. What was it, Anne? The Knave of Diamonds on a black mare, riding to perdition?"

He laughed at her softly, as though she were a child. He was still watching her hands. Suddenly he laid his own upon them and looked into her face.

"Or was it just a savage?" he asked her quietly.

Against her will, in spite of the blaze of sunshine, she shivered.

"Yes," he said. "But isn't it better to face him

than to run away? Haven't you always found it so? You kissed him once, Anne. Do you remember? It was the greatest thing that ever happened to him."

He spoke with a gentleness that amazed her. His eyes held hers, but without compulsion. He was lulling her fear of him to rest, as he alone knew how.

"I have wondered since if I did wrong," she answered, with quivering lips.

"Then don't wonder," he said. "For I was nearer to the God you worship at that moment than I had ever been before. I never believed in Him till then, but that night I wrestled with Him, and got beaten."

There was silence before he asked:

"Have you had enough of this? Shall we move on?"

She rose, and as they reached the car she laid her hand for an instant on his arm.

"If it did that for you, Nap," she said, "I do not regret it."

He smiled in his faint, cynical fashion.

"I believe you'll turn me out a good man someday," he said. "And I wonder if you will like me any when it's done."

"I only want you to be your better self," she answered gently.

"Which is a myth, which exists only in your most gracious imagination," he replied as he handed her in.

It was nearly two before they reached Bramhurst and drew up before one ancient Inn. Upstairs, in a lattice-windowed room with sloping floor and bulging ceiling, a room that was full of the scent of honeysuckle, Anne washed away the dust of the road.

Descending, she found Nap waiting for her in the oak-beamed coffee-room. He made her sit facing the open window, looking forth upon hill and forest and shallow winding river.

The stout old English waiter who attended to their wants very speedily withdrew.

"He thinks we are on our wedding-trip," said Nap.

She glanced at him sharply.

"Yes, I let him have it so!" he returned. "I never destroy a pretty illusion if I can help it."

"What time do we start back?" said Anne, aware of burning cheeks, which he was studying with amusement.

"Would you like some ice?" he suggested.

She laughed, with something of an effort. "Don't be ridiculous, Nap!"

"I am sure you have never done anything so improper in all your life before," he went on. "What must it feel like? P'r'aps you would have preferred me to explain the situation to him in detail? There is only one remedy that I can suggest, and that is to pretend it's true."

"I am not good at pretending," Anne answered gravely.

"Very true, O Queen!" He laughed. "Horribly true! But I am, you know, a positive genius in that respect. So I'm going to pretend I'm an Englishman, of the worthy, thick-headed, bull-dog breed.

"And you are my devoted and adorable wife. You needn't look shocked. It's all for the sake of that chap's morals. Do you think I can do it?"

"I don't want you to do it, Nap," she said earnestly.

He dropped the subject instantly.

"Your wish is law. There is only one other person in this world who can command my implicit obedience in this fashion. So I hope you appreciate your power."

"And that other is Lucas?" said Anne.

"Luke the irresistible! Did you ever try to resist him?"

She shook her head, with a smile.

"Take my advice then," he said. "Never do! He could whip creation with his hands tied behind him."

* * *

Finishing luncheon, they went out over the common that stretched from the very door, down the hillside of short, sun-baked grass, passing between masses of scorched broom, till they came to the green shade of forest trees and the gleam of a running stream.

Anne stopped on the edge of the stream. Wonderful dragon-flies such as she had never seen before, peacock, orange, and palest green, darted to and fro above the brown water.

"Am I in fairyland, I wonder?" she asked.

"Or the Garden of Eden."

She laughed a little, and stooping tried to reach

a forget-me-not that grew on the edge of the water.

"Beware of the serpent!" he warned. "Anyway, don't tumble in!"

She stretched back a hand to him.

"Don't let me go!"

His hand closed instantly and firmly upon her wrist and in a moment she drew back with the flower in her hand.

"Ought we not to be starting back?" she asked.

"It won't be so hot in half an hour."

"But how long will it take?"

"It can be done in under three hours. If we start at half past four you should be home well before sunset."

He smiled with the words, and Anne suffered herself to be persuaded. Certainly the shade of the beech trees was infinitely preferable to the glare of the dusty roads, and the slumberous atmosphere made her feel undeniably languorous.

She sat down therefore on the roots of a tree, still watching the dragon-flies flitting above the water.

Nap stripped off his coat and made it into a cushion.

"Lean back on this. Yes, really. I'm thankful for the excuse to go without it. How is that? Comfortable?"

She thanked him with a smile.

"I mustn't go to sleep,"

"Why not?" said Nap. "There is nothing to disturb you. I'm going back to the Inn to order tea before we start."

She leaned back with a sense of complete well-being and closed her eyes. . . .

When she opened them again it was with a guilty feeling of having been asleep for a long time. With a start she sat up and looked round her.

The sun-rays were still slanting through the wood, but dully, as though they shone through a sheet of smoked glass. The stillness was intense.

A sharp sense of nervousness pricked her. There seemed to be something ominous in the atmosphere; or was it only in her own heart that it existed? And where was Nap? Surely he had been gone for a very long time!

She rose stiffly and picked up his coat. At the same instant a shrill whistle sounded through the wood, and in a moment she saw him coming swiftly towards her.

Quietly she moved to meet him. He began to speak before he reached her.

"I was afraid you would be tired of waiting and wander about till you got frightened and lost yourself. Do you ever have hysterics?"

"Never," said Anne firmly.

"Well, that's a weight off my mind, anyway," he remarked at length. "For I have a staggering piece of news for you which I hardly dare to impart. Oh, it's no good looking at your watch. It's hopelessly late, nearly six o'clock, and in any case I can't get you home tonight. There's no petrol."

"Nap!"

"Take it nicely!" he pleaded. "I know I was an all-fired fool not to see to it for myself. But I was called away and so I had to leave it to those dunderheads at the garage. I only made the discovery when I left you a couple of hours ago.

"There was just enough left to take me to Rodding, so I pelted off at once to some motor-works I knew there, only to find I couldn't get a conveyance anywhere. So I just put up the motor and came back across country on foot. I don't see what else I could have done.

"My only consolation," he went on, "is that you have your clothes with you, which is more than I have. Oh, yes, I had the sense to think of that contingency. Your bag is at the Inn here, waiting for you."

"You should have taken me back with you to Rodding," Anne said.

"Yes, I know. But I expected to be back in half an hour if all went well. It's easy to be wise after the event, isn't it? I've thought of that myself since. Anyway, there is some tea waiting for us. Shall we go back?"

"Then what do you propose to do?"

"Nothing before morning, I'm afraid. Then we can take the train from Rodding to Staps, where I can get some petrol. We ought by that means to reach home sometime in the afternoon. It is the only feasible plan, I am afraid; unless you can suggest a better one."

Anne walked for several seconds in silence.

"Would it be quite impossible to walk to Rodding now?" she asked.

"Not at all," said Nap. "It is about eight miles

through the woods. We should be benighted, of course. Also I fancy there is a storm coming up. But if you wish to make the attempt . . ."

"I was only wondering," she said quietly, "if we could get an evening train to Staps. That, I know, is on the main line. You could put up there, and I could take the night train to town."

"Shall we have tea before we start?" Nap asked.

Anne gave an uneasy glance at the sky.

"I believe you are right about the storm," she said.

"I generally am."

"I shouldn't like to be benighted in the woods," she said presently.

His scoffing smile showed for an instant.

"Alone with me, too! Most improper!"

"I was thinking we might miss the way," Anne returned with dignity. "I wonder . . . shall we risk it?"

She turned to him as if consulting him.

"That is for you to decide," he said. "We might do it. The storm won't break at present."

"It will be violent when it does," she said.

"It will," he nodded.

She quickened her steps instinctively, and he lengthened his stride. The smile had ceased to twitch his lips.

"Have you decided?" he asked her suddenly, and his voice sounded almost stern.

They were nearing the top of the hill. She paused, panting a little.

"Yes. I will spend the night here."

He gave her a glance of approval.

"You are a wise woman."

"I hope so," said Anne. "I must telegraph at once to Dimsdale and tell him not to expect me."

Nap's glance fell away from her. He said nothing whatever.

* * *

"Thank the gods, we are the only guests!" Nap said that evening, as they sat down to dine at the table at which they had lunched.

Afterwards Nap opened a window that led into a miniature rose-garden. Beyond stretched the common, every detail standing out with marvellous vividness in the weird light of the approaching storm.

"St. Christopher!" he murmured softly. "We are going to catch it!"

Anne sat down in a low chair near him, her chin on her hand. He turned a little and looked down at her, and thus some minutes slipped away, the man as tensely still as the awe-stricken world.

He moved at last with a curious gesture as if he freed and restrained himself by the same action.

"Why don't you think out aloud?" he said.

She raised her eyes for a moment.

"I was thinking of my husband," she said.

He made a sharp movement, a movement that was almost fierce, and again seemed to take a fresh grip upon himself. His black brows met above his brooding eyes.

"Can't you leave him out of the reckoning for this one night?" he asked.

"I think not," she answered quietly.

He turned his face to the sinking sun. It shone like a smouldering furnace behind bars of inky cloud.

"You told me once," he said, speaking with obvious constraint, "that you did not think you would ever live with him again."

"I thought so then."

"And what has happened to make you change your mind?"

Anne was silent. She could have seen the fire that leapt and darted in the dusky eyes had she been looking at him, but her chin was back upon her hand. She was gazing out into the darkening world with the eyes of a woman who sees once more departed visions.

"I think," she said slowly, at length, as he waited immovably for her answer, "that I see my duty more clearly now than then."

"Duty! Duty!" he said impatiently. "Duty is your fetish. You sacrifice your whole life to it. And what do you get in return? A sense of virtue perhaps, nothing more. There isn't much warming power in virtue. I've tried it and I know!"

He broke off to utter a very bitter laugh.

"And so I've given it up. It's a trail that leads to nowhere."

"I hoped you might come to think otherwise."

He shrugged his shoulders.

"How can I? I've lived the life of a saint for the past six months, and I am no nearer heaven than when I began. It's too slow a process for me. I wasn't made to plough an endless furrow."

"We all of us say that," said Anne, with her faint smile. "But do any of us really know what we were made for? Are we not all in the making still?"

"I can't be abstruse tonight. I know what I was made for, and I know what you were made for."

Anne uttered a little sigh.

"I wish the storm would break," she said. "I am tired of waiting."

As if in answer, out of the west there rose a long, low rumble.

For as if the signal had come, Nap turned with a movement incredibly swift, a movement that was almost a spring, and caught her up into his arms.

"Are you tired of waiting, my Queen, my Queen?" he said, and there was a note of fierce laughter in his words. "Then, by heaven, you shall wait no longer!"

His quick breath scorched her face, and in a moment almost before she knew what was happening his lips were on her own. He kissed her as she had never been kissed before, a single fiery kiss that sent all the blood in tumult to her heart.

She shrank and quivered under it, but she was powerless to escape. There was sheer unshackled savagery in the holding of his arms, and dismay thrilled her through and through.

Yet, as his lips left hers, she managed to speak, though her voice was no more than a gasping whisper.

"Nap, are you mad? Let me go!"

But he only held her faster, faster still.

"Yes, I am mad," he said, and the words came quick and passionate. "I am mad for you, Anne. I worship you. And I swear that while I live no other man shall ever hold you in his arms again. Ann, goddess, queen, woman, you are mine, you are mine, you are mine!"

Again his lips pressed hers, and again from head to foot she felt as if a flame had scorched her. Desperately she began to resist him, though terribly conscious that he had her at his mercy.

But he quelled her resistance instantly, with a mastery that made her know more thoroughly her utter impotence.

"Do you think that you can hold me in check forever?" he said. "I tell you it only makes me worse. I am a savage, and chains of that sort won't hold me. What is the good of fighting against fate?

"You have done it as long as I have known you; but you are beaten at last. Oh, you may turn your face from me. It makes no difference now. I've played for this, and I've won! You have been goddess to me ever since the day I met you. Tonight, you shall be woman!"

He broke into a low, exultant laugh. She could feel the fierce beating of his heart, and her own died within her. The blaze of his passion ringed her round like a forest fire in which all things perish.

But even then she knew that somewhere, somewhere, there was a way of escape, and with the instinct of the hunted creature she sought it.

"Tonight," she said, "I shall know whether you have ever really loved me."

"What?" he said. "You dare to question that now? Do you want to put me to the proof then? Shall I show you how much I love you?"

"No," she said. "Take your arms away!"

She did not expect his obedience, but on the instant he spread them wide and released her.

"And now?" he said.

She almost tottered, so amazing had been his compliance. And then as swiftly came the knowledge that he had not really set her free. It had pleased him to humour her, that was all.

He stood before her with all the arrogance of a conqueror. And through the gathering darkness his eyes shone like the eyes of a tiger, two flames piercing the gloom.

She mustered all her strength to face him, confronting him with that unconscious majesty that first had drawn him to her.

"And now," she said, "let us once and for all understand one another."

"What?" he said. "Don't you understand me yet? Don't you realise, yet, that when a man of my stamp wants a woman he—takes her?"

Again there throbbed in his voice that deep

note of savagery, such savagery as made her quail. But it was no moment for shrinking. She knew instinctively that at the first sign of weakness he would take her back into his arms.

She straightened herself therefore, summoning all her pride.

"Do you really think I am the sort of woman to be taken so?" she asked. "Do you really think I am yours for the taking? If so, then you have never known me. Nor, till this moment, have I known you."

He heard her without the faintest hint of astonishment or shame, standing before her with that careless animal grace of his that made him in some fashion superb.

"Yes," he said, "I really do think you are mine for the taking this time, but you will admit I've been patient. And I've taken the trouble to make things easy for you. I've spirited you away without putting you through any ordeals of hesitation or suspense.

"I've done it all quite unobtrusively. Tomorrow we go to London, after that to Paris, and after that—whithersoever you will—anywhere under the sun where we can be alone. As to knowing each other . . ."

His voice changed subtly, became soft, with something of a purring quality.

"We have all our lives before us, and we shall be learning every day."

His absolute assurance struck her dumb. There was something implacable about it, something unassailable—a stronghold which she felt powerless to attack.

"Doesn't that programme attract you?" he said, drawing nearer to her. "Can you suggest a better one? The whole world is before us. Shall we go exploring, you and I, alone in the wilds, and find some Eden that no man has ever trodden before?

"Shall we, Anne? Right away from everywhere, somewhere in the sun, where I can teach you to be happy and you can teach me to be—good."

But at his movement she moved also, drawing back.

"No!" she said. "You are building upon a false foundation. If it were not so, I don't think I could possibly forgive you. As it is, I think when you realise your mistake you will find it hard to forgive yourself. I have treated you as a friend because I thought I could do so with safety.

"I thought for the sake of my friendship you had given up all thought of anything else. I thought you were to be trusted, and I trusted you. Oh, I admit I ought to have known you better. But I shall never make that mistake again."

"No," Nap said. "I don't think you will."

He spoke deliberately; he almost drawled. Yet a sense of danger stabbed her. His sudden coldness was more terrible than his heat.

"But why say this to me now?" he said. "Do you think it will make any difference?"

He had not moved as he uttered the words, and

yet she felt as if he menaced her. He made her think of a crouching tiger, a tiger whose devotion had turned to sudden animosity.

She did not shrink from him, but her heart quickened.

"It must make a difference," she said. "You have utterly misunderstood me, or you would never have brought me here."

"Don't be too sure of that," he returned. "It may be that you can deceive yourself more easily than you can deceive me. Or again, it may be that I have come to the end of my patience and have decided to take by storm what cannot be won by waiting."

She drew herself up proudly.

"And you call that . . . love!" she said, with a scorn that she had never before turned against him. "You dare to call that . . . love!"

"Call it what you will!" he flashed back. "It is something that can crush your cold virtue into atoms, something that can turn you from a marble saint into a living woman of flesh and blood. For your sake, I've tried, I've agonised, to reach your level. And I've failed because I can't breathe there.

"Tonight you shall come down from your heights to mine. You who have never lived yet shall know life, as I know it, tonight!"

Fiercely he flung the words, and the breath of his passion was like a fiery blast blown from the heart of a raging furnace. But still she did not shrink before him. Proud and calm, she waited, bearing herself with a queenly courage that never faltered.

And it was as if she stood in a magic circle, for he raised no hand to touch her. Without word or movement she kept him at bay. Erect, unflinching, regal, she held her own.

He caught his breath as he faced her. The beast in him slunk back afraid, but the devil urged him forward. He came close to her, peering into her face, searching for that weak place in every woman's armour which the devil generally knows how to find.

Still he did not offer to touch her. He had let her go out of his arms when he had believed her his own, and now he could not take her again.

"Anne," he said suddenly, "where is your love for me? I will swear you loved me once."

"I never loved you," she answered, her words clear-cut, cold as steel. "I never loved you. Once, it is true, I fancied that you were such a man as I could have loved. But that passed. I did not know you in those days. I know you now."

"And hate me for what you know?" he said.

"No," she answered. "I do not even hate you."

"What then?" he gibed. "You are—sorry for me, perhaps?"

"No!" Very distinct and steady came her reply. "I only despise you."

"What?" he exclaimed.

"I despise you," she repeated slowly, "knowing what you might be, and knowing . . . what you are."

The words passed out in silence, a silence so tense that it seemed as if the world itself had stopped. Through it after many seconds came Nap's voice, so softly that it scarcely seemed to break it.

"It is not always wise to despise an enemy, Lady Carfax, especially if you chance to be in that enemy's power."

He drew something abruptly from his pocket and held it up before her.

"Do you see this?"

She stirred then, ever so slightly, a movement wholly involuntary, instantly checked.

"Are you going to shoot me?"

"I thought that would make you speak," he remarked. "And you still despise me?"

Her breathing had quickened, but her answer was instant; for the first time it held a throb of anger.

"I despise you for a coward. You are even viler than I thought."

He returned the weapon to his pocket.

"It is not for you," he said. "I am more primitive than that. It is for the man who stands between us, for the man who thought he could whip Nap Errol, and live. I have never gone unarmed since."

He paused a moment, grimly regarding her.

"There is only one thing I will take in exchange for that man's life," he said. "Only—one—thing!"

But she stood like a statue, uttering no word.

A sudden gust of passion swept over him, lashing him to headlong fury.

"And that one thing I mean to have! No power in heaven or hell shall keep you from me."

His voice rose, and in the darkness those two flames glowed more redly, such flames as had surely never burned before in the face of a man.

"Whatever you may say, you are mine, and in your heart you know it. Sooner or later, sooner or later, I will make you own it."

His voice sank suddenly to a whisper, no longer passionate, only inexpressibly evil.

"Will you despise me then, Queen Anne? I wonder—I wonder!"

She moved at last, raised her hand, stiffly pointed.

"Go!" she said. "Go!"

Yet for a space he still stood in the doorway, menacing her, a vital figure, lithe, erect, dominant. The tension was terrible. It seemed to be strained to the snapping point, and yet it held.

It was the fiercest battle she had ever known, a battle in which his will grappled with hers in a mighty, all-mastering grip, increasing every instant till she felt crushed, impotent, lost, as if all the powers of evil were let loose and seething round her, dragging her down.

Her resolution began to falter. She became conscious of a numbing sense of physical weakness, an oppression so overwhelming that she thought her heart would never beat again.

Once more she seemed to totter on the edge of a depth too immense to contemplate, to hover above the very pit of destruction. . . .

Then suddenly the ordeal was over. A blinding flash of lightning lit the room, glimmered weirdly, splitting the gloom as a sword rending a curtain, and was gone. There came a sound like the snarl of a startled animal, and the next instant a frightful crash of thunder.

Anne reeled back, dazed, stunned, utterly unnerved, and sank into a chair.

When she came to herself she was alone.

Chapter Five

A puff of rain-washed air wandered in through the wide-flung window, and Lucas Errol turned his head languidly upon the pillow to feel it on his face.

"What is it, Bertie?" he asked.

"It's an infernal shame to worry you when you're not fit for it!" Bertie replied. "But the mother and I both think you ought to know."

"Go ahead, dear fellow! It's Nap, isn't it? What has become of him?"

"That's just the question. You know he went off in the car with Lady Carfax yesterday morning?"

"I didn't know," murmured Lucas.

"Late last night the car had not returned, and the mother began to wonder, and in the end I posted off to the Manor to know if she had arrived. She had not.

"But while I was there a wire came for the butler from a place called Bramhurst, which is about fifty miles away, to say that the car had broken down and they couldn't return before today. Well, that looked to me deuced queer. I'm convinced that Nap is up to some devilry.

"We couldn't rest, either of us. And in the end Mother ordered the big Daimler and went off to Bramhurst herself."

"She is not back yet?" Lucas asked.

"No. But Nap was in a wild-beast mood before they started. He nearly rode the black mare to death in the early morning."

"Why wasn't I told of that?" Lucas opened his eyes with the question and looked directly at his brother's worried countenance.

"My dear fellow, you were too sick to be bothered. Besides, you were taking morphia. He saw to that."

"Bertie," Lucas said, "go down to the garage and leave word that as soon as Nap returns I want to speak to him."

"He won't return," said Bertie, with conviction.

"I think he will. It is even possible that he has returned already. In any case, go and tell them. Tawny, what is it?"

The valet came to his master's side.

"A note, Sir, from the Manor."

"Who brought it?" asked Lucas.

"A groom, Sir."

"Waiting for an answer?"

"Yes, Sir."

Lucas opened the note. It was from Anne.

He read a few lines, then glanced at Bertie.

"It's all right, Bertie. Go and give that message, will you? Say it's important—an urgent matter of business."

Bertie departed, and Lucas's eyes returned to the sheet he held.

"Pen and paper, Tawny! Now put your arm behind the pillows and give me a hoist. Slowly now, slowly!"

And then, as the man supported him, very slowly and unsteadily he traced a few words:

"Don't worry. All's well. *Lucas.*"

Abruptly the pen fell from his fingers; his head dropped back. His face was drawn and ghastly as he uttered a few gasping whispers. "Tawny, give me something—quick! This pain is—killing me!"

Then he knew without turning that someone had entered, and he betrayed no surprise when Nap's hand suddenly whisked the glass from his valet's hold and held it to the panting lips.

When he could speak Lucas said:

"No morphia! Don't go away, Boney, I want you."

"So I've been told. I am quite at your service. Don't speak till you feel better."

"Ah! I am better now. There's magic about you, I believe. Or is it electricity?"

"Is Hudson to take this note? Can I address it for you?"

"Yes, to Lady Carfax at the Manor. It is to go at once."

Nap thrust it into an envelope with a perfectly inscrutable countenance, scrawled the address, and handed it to the valet.

Then he pulled up a chair near his brother.

"Now, what ails the great Chief? Does he think his brother will run away while he sleeps?"

There was a hint of tenderness underlying the banter in his voice. He stooped with the words and picked up a letter that lay on the floor.

"This yours?"

"You may read it."

"Many thanks! I don't read women's letters unless they chance to be addressed to me—no, not even if they concern me very nearly."

He laid the letter on the bed within reach of his brother's hand.

"That ranch in Arizona, Boney, is beginning to worry me," Lucas said slowly. "I want you to take it in hand. It's a little job peculiarly suited to your abilities."

"What do you know of my abilities?"

"More than most." Very steadily Lucas made answer. "I depend on you in a fashion you little dream of, and I guess you won't fail me."

Nap's jaw slowly hardened.

"I'm not very likely to disappoint you," he observed, "more especially as I have no intention of removing to Arizona at present."

"Not if I make a point of it?" Lucas spoke heavily, as if the effort of speech was great. His hand had clenched upon Anne's letter.

Nap leaned forward without replying, and looked at him attentively.

"Yes," Lucas said very wearily. "It has come to that. I can't have you here disturbing the public peace. I won't have my own brother arraigned as a murderer. Nor will I have Anne Carfax pilloried because of you for all England to throw mud at. I've stood a good deal from you, Boney, but I'm damned if I'm going to stand this."

"The only question is, can you prevent it?" said Nap, without the faintest change of countenance.

"I am going to prevent it."

"If you can."

"I am going to prevent it," Lucas repeated. "Before we go any further, give me that shooter of yours."

Nap hesitated for a single instant, then, with a gesture openly contemptuous, he took the revolver from his pocket and tossed it onto the bed.

"Now, I want you to tell me something," Lucas said. "I seem to remember your saying to me once in this very room that you and Lady Carfax were friends, no more, no less. You were mighty anxious that I shouldn't misunderstand. Remember that episode?"

"Perfectly," said Nap.

"I surmised that you told me that because you honestly cared for her as a friend. Was that so?"

"You may say so if you wish," he said.

"Meaning that things have changed since then?" questioned Lucas, in his tired drawl.

"You can put it how you like. You can say, if you like, that I am a bigger blackguard now than I was then. It makes no difference how you put it."

"But I want to know," said Lucas quietly. "Are you a blackguard, Boney?"

His eyes were fixed steadily upon the dusky face with its prominent cheek-bones and mocking mouth. Perhaps he knew what Anne had discovered long before—that those sensitive lips might easily reveal what the fierce eyes hid.

"A matter of opinion," threw back Nap. "If I am, Anne Carfax has made me so."

"Anne Carfax," said Lucas very deliberately, "has done her best to make a man of you. It is not her fault if she has failed. It is not her fault that you have chosen to drag her friendship through the mire."

"Friendship!" broke in Nap. "She gave me more than that."

"Whatever she gave you was the gift of a good woman, of which you have proved yourself utterly unworthy."

Nap sprang to his feet.

"Be it so!" he exclaimed harshly. "I am unworthy. What of it? She always knew I was."

"Yet she trusted you."

"She trusted me, yes. Having cast out the devil she found in possession, she thought there was nothing more to me. She thought that I should be content to wander empty all my days through dry places, seeking rest. She forgot the sequel, forgot what was bound to happen when I found none."

He flung his arms wide with a sudden, passionate laugh.

"Why, my good fellow, I'd sooner rank myself with the beasts that perish. And I'd sooner perish too; yes, die with a rope round my throat in the good old English fashion. There's nothing in that. I'd as soon die that way as any other."

"Do you mind sitting down?" said Lucas.

Nap looked at him sharply.

"Sit down," Lucas reiterated. "Now will you take the trouble to make me understand what exactly are your present intentions, and why?"

"Doesn't that letter tell you?" said Nap.

"This letter," Lucas answered, "is the desperate appeal of a very unhappy woman who is in mortal dread of you murdering her husband."

"That all?" said Nap. The red glare of savagery flickered for an instant in his eyes. "She has no fears on her own account then?"

"Will you explain?"

"Oh, certainly, if you need explanation. I mean that the death of Sir Giles Carfax is no more than a stepping-stone, a means to an end. So long as he lives, he will stand in my way. Therefore, Sir Giles will go. And mark me, any other man who attempts to come between us I will kill also.

"Heaven knows what there is in her, something I have never seen in any other woman, something that goes to my head. She has driven me mad, and I warn you—I warn you—you had better not interfere with me!"

He flung the words like a challenge. His lower jaw was thrust forward. He looked like a savage animal menacing his keeper.

But Lucas lay without moving a muscle, lay still and quiet, without tension and without emotion of any description, simply watching, as a disinterested spectator might watch, the fiery rebellion that had kindled against him.

At length very deliberately he held out the revolver.

"Well," he drawled, "my life isn't worth much, it's true. And you are quite welcome to take your gun and end it here and now if you feel so disposed. For I warn you, Nap Errol, you'll find me considerably more in your way than Sir Giles Carfax or any other man. I stand between you already, and while I live you won't shunt me."

Nap's lips showed their scoffing smile.

"Unfortunately, or otherwise, you are out of the reckoning," he said.

"Am I? And how long have I been that?"

Nap was silent. He looked suddenly stubborn.

Lucas waited. There was even a hint of humour in his steady eyes.

"And that's where you begin to make a mistake," he said presently. "You're a poor sort of blackguard at best, Boney, and that's why you can't break away. Take this thing. I've no use for it. But maybe in Arizona you'll find it advisable to carry arms. Come over here and read the letter."

But Nap swung away with a gesture of fierce unrest. He fell to prowling to and fro, stopping short of the bed at each turn, refusing doggedly to face the quiet eyes of the man who lay there.

Minutes passed. Lucas was still watching, but he was no longer at his ease. His brows were drawn heavily. He looked like a man undergoing torture. His hand was still fast closed upon Anne's letter.

He spoke at last, seeming to grind out the words through clenched teeth.

"I guess there's no help for it, Boney. We've figured it out before, you and I. I'm no great swell at fighting, but—I can hold my own against you. And if it comes to a tug-of-war—you'll lose."

Nap came to his side at last and stood there, still not looking at him.

"You seem almighty sure of that," he said.

"That's so," said Lucas simply. "And if you

care to know why, I'll tell you. It's just because your heart isn't in it. One half of you is on my side. You're just not blackguard enough."

"And so you want to send me to Arizona to mature?" suggested Nap grimly.

"Or to find yourself," Lucas substituted. "Say, Boney, if you don't give in pretty soon I'll make you take me along."

"You!" Nap's eyes came down at last to the drawn face. He gave a slight start. "If Capper were here he'd say I was killing you. For heaven's sake, man, rest!"

"No," gasped Lucas. "No! I haven't finished —yet. Boney, you—you've got to listen. There's no quarrel between us. Only, if you will be so damned headstrong, I must be headstrong too. I mean what I say. If you won't go to Arizona alone, you will go with me. And we'll start tonight."

He paused.

"Give it up, Boney!" he said at last. "I'll go with you to the ends of the earth sooner than let you do this thing, and you'll find me a very considerable encumbrance. Do you honestly believe yourself capable of shunting me at will?"

"I honestly believe you'll kill yourself if you don't rest," Nap said.

He looked down suddenly into the tired eyes. The fierce glare had gone utterly out of his own. His very pose had altered.

"Then I shall die in a good cause," Lucas murmured, with the ghost of a smile. "You needn't say any more, Boney. I guess I shall rest now."

"Because you think you've beaten me," Nap said curtly.

"Guess it's your victory, dear fellow, not mine," Lucas answered very gently.

A gleam that was not a smile crossed the harsh face, softening but not gladdening it.

"It's a mighty hollow one anyway. And I'm not going for nothing, not even to please you."

"Anything—to the half of my kingdom," Lucas said.

Nap sat down on the edge of the bed. The madness had passed, or he had thrust it back out of sight in the darkest recesses of his soul. He laid a hand upon his brother's arm and felt it speculatively.

"No sinew, no flesh, and scarcely any blood!" he said. "And yet!"—his mouth twisted—"my master! Luke, you're a genius!"

"Oh, shucks, Boney! What's brute strength anyway?"

"Not much," Nap admitted. "But you—you haven't the force of a day-old puppy. Maybe, when I'm out of the way fighting my devils in the desert, you'll give Capper a free hand, and let him make of you what you were always intended to be—a human masterpiece. There won't be any obstacles when I'm out of the way."

Lucas's hand felt for and closed upon his.

"If that's your condition, it's a bargain," he said simply.

"And you'll put up a fight for it, eh, Luke? You're rather apt to slack when I'm not by."

A very tender look came into the elder man's eyes.

"With God's help, Boney," he said, "I'll pull through."

Nap rose as if that ended the interview. Yet rising he still gripped the weak hand of the man who was his master.

A moment he stood, then suddenly bent very low and touched it with his forehead.

"I leave tonight," he said, and turning went very quickly and noiselessly from the room.

* * *

It was a very cheery Dot Waring who ran across the wet fields that afternoon to the Manor to see Lady Carfax. But it was something of a disappointment to be met by old Dimsdale with the intelligence that Her Ladyship was very tired and resting.

He added, seeing Dot's face fall, that Mrs. Errol was spending a few days at the Manor and would no doubt be very pleased to see her.

"Yes, dear Anne's in bed," Mrs. Errol said. "She and Nap went for a motor ride yesterday, and broke down and were benighted. Nap always was sort of reckless.

"We had a message late last night telling us what had happened, and I went off at once in the big car and brought Anne home. Nap had to wait for his own car, but I guess he's back by this time. And poor Anne was so worn out when we got back that I persuaded her to go to bed right away."

When Dot left, her way lay over the shoulder

of a hill, that same hill on which Sir Giles Carfax had once wreaked his mad vengeance upon his enemy. There she caught sight of something she had not expected to see in the valley below her.

A dark object, curiously shapeless, that yet had the look of an animal, was lying in a hollow, and over it bent the figure of a man.

Dot's heart quickened a little. Had there been an accident? she asked herself. She hastened her steps and drew near.

As she did so, the man straightened himself suddenly, and turned round, and instantly a thrill of recognition and of horror went through the girl. It was Nap Errol, and the thing on the ground was his black mare.

She knew in a flash what had happened. Bertie had predicted disaster too often for her not to know. A great wave of repulsion surged through her. She was for the moment too horrified for speech.

Nap stood erect, motionless, waiting for her. There was a terrible set smile on his face like the smile on a death-mask. He did not utter a word as she came up.

The mare was quite dead. The starting, blood-shot eyes were already glazed. She lay in a huddled heap, mud-stained, froth-splashed, with blood upon her flanks.

White-faced and speechless, Dot stood and looked. It was the first time that tragedy had ever touched her gay young life.

She stooped at last, and with trembling, pitiful

fingers touched the velvet muzzle. Then suddenly indignation, fierce, overwhelming, headlong, swept over her, crowding out even her horror. She stood up and faced Nap in such a tornado of fury as had never before shaken her.

"You brute!" she said. "You fiend! You . . . you . . ."

"Devil," said Nap. "Why not say it? I shan't contradict you."

He spoke quite quietly, so quietly that even in the wild tempest of her anger she was awed.

There was something unfathomable about him, something that nevertheless arrested her at the very height of her fury. His manner was so still, so deadly still, and so utterly free from cynicism.

She stood and stared at him, a queer sensation of dread making her very heart feel cold.

"I should go if I were you," he said.

But Dot stood still, as if struck powerless.

"You can't do any good," he went on, his tone quite gentle, even remotely kind. "I had to kill something, but it was a pity you chanced to see it. You had better go home and forget it."

Dot's white lips began to move, but it was several seconds before any sound came from them.

"What are you going to do?"

"That's my affair."

He was still faintly smiling, but his smile appalled her. It was so cold, so impersonal, so void of all vitality.

"Really, you had better go," he said.

But Dot's dread had begun to take tangible

form. Perhaps the very shock she had undergone had served to awaken in her some of the dormant instincts of her womanhood.

She stood her ground, obedient to an inner prompting that she dared not ignore.

"Will you . . . walk a little way with me?" she said at last.

For the first time Nap's eyes looked at her intently, searched her closely, unsparingly. She faced the scrutiny bravely, but she trembled under it.

"Are you going to faint?" he said after a lengthy pause.

"No," she answered quickly. "I never faint. Only . . . only . . . I do feel . . . rather sick."

He put his hand under her arm with a suddenness that allowed no protest and began to march her up the hill.

Long before they reached the top, Dot's face was scarlet with exertion and she was gasping painfully for breath; but he would not let her rest till they were over the summit and out of sight of the valley and what lay there.

Then, to her relief, he stopped.

"Better now?"

"Yes!" she said, panting.

His hands fell away from her. He turned to go. But swiftly she turned also and caught his arm.

"Nap, please . . ." she begged, "please . . ."

He stood still, and again his eyes scanned her.

"Yes?"

The brief word sounded stern, but Dot was too anxious to take any note of that.

"Come a little further," she urged. "It . . . it's lonely through the wood."

"What are you afraid of?" said Nap.

She could not tell him the truth, and she hesitated to lie. But his eyes read her through and through without effort.

When he turned and walked beside her she was quite sure that he had fathomed the unspeakable dread which had been steadily growing within her since the moment of their meeting.

He vaulted the stile into the wood, and held up his hand to her. As she placed hers within it she summoned her resolution, and spoke.

"Nap, I'm sorry I said what I did just now."

He raised his brows for a fraction of a second.

"I forget what you said."

She flushed a little.

"Because you don't choose to remember. But I am sorry I spoke, all the same. I lost my temper, and I . . . I suppose I had no right to."

"Pray don't apologise," he said.

"Nap," she said, standing still with her hands nervously clasped behind her, "please don't think me . . . impertinent, or anything of that sort. But I can't help knowing that you are feeling pretty bad about it. And . . . and . . . I know you are not a brute really. You didn't mean to do it."

A curious little smile came into Nap's face.

"It's good of you to make excuses for me," he observed. "You happen to know me rather well, don't you?"

"I know you are in trouble," she answered, rather piteously. "And . . . I'm sorry."

"Thanks!" he said. "Do we part here?"

She thrust out her hand impulsively.

"I thought we decided to be . . . friends," she said, a sharp quiver in her voice.

"Well?" Nap asked.

Dot was on the verge of tears. She choked them back desperately.

"You might behave as if we were," she said.

"I'm not friends with anyone at the present moment," he said. "But it isn't worth crying over anyway. Why don't you run home and play draughts with Bertie?"

"Because I'm not what you take me for! I can't help what you think of me," she said rather breathlessly. "But I'm not going to leave you here by yourself. You may be as furious as you like. I simply won't!"

She thought for the moment that he actually was furious and braced herself to meet the tempest of his wrath. And then to her amazement he spoke in a tone that held neither sarcasm nor resentment, only a detached sort of curiosity.

"Are you quite sure I'm worth all this trouble?"

"Quite sure," she answered emphatically.

"And I wonder how you arrived at that conclusion," he said, with a twist of the mouth that was scarcely humourous.

She did not answer, for she felt utterly unequal to the discussion.

They began to walk on down the mossy pathway. Suddenly an idea came to Dot.

"I only wish Lady Carfax were here," she exclaimed impetuously. "She would know how to convince you of that."

"Would she?" said Nap. He shot a swift look at the girl beside him, then: "Lady Carfax has thrown me over."

Dot gave a great start.

"Oh, surely not! She would never throw over anyone. And you have always been such friends."

"Till I offended her," said Nap.

"Oh, but couldn't you go and apologise?" urged Dot eagerly. "She is so sweet. I know she would forgive anybody."

He jerked up his head.

"I don't happen to want her forgiveness. And even if I did, I shouldn't ask for it. I'm not particularly great at humbling myself."

"Isn't that rather a mistake?" said Dot.

"No," he rejoined briefly. "Not when I'm despised already for a savage and the descendant of savages."

"I am afraid I don't understand," she said.

He uttered a sudden harsh laugh.

"I see you don't. Or you would be despising me too."

"I shall never do that," she said quickly.

He looked at her again, still with a mocking smile upon his lips. He bore himself with a certain royal pride that made her feel decidedly small.

"You will never say that again," he remarked.

"Why not?" she demanded.

"Because," he answered, with a drawling sneer, "you are like the rest of creation. You put breed before everything. Unless a man has what you are pleased to term 'pure blood' in his veins, he is beyond the pale."

"Whatever are you talking about?" said Dot, frankly mystified.

He stopped dead and faced her.

"I am talking of myself, if you want to know," he told her very bitterly. "I am beyond the pale, an illegitimate son, with a strain of Red Indian in my veins to complete my damnation."

"Good gracious!" said Dot.

She stared at him for a few seconds mutely, as if the sudden announcement had taken her breath away.

"Then . . . then . . . Mrs. Errol . . ." she stammered.

"Is not my mother," he informed her grimly. "Did you ever seriously think she was?" He flung back his shoulders arrogantly. "You're almost blind, you English."

Dot continued to contemplate him with her frank eyes, as if viewing for the first time a specimen of some rarity.

"Well, I don't see that it makes any difference," she said at length. "You are you just the same. I . . . I really don't see quite why you told me."

"No?" said Nap, staring back at her with eyes

that told her nothing. "P'r'aps I just wanted to show you that you are wasting your solicitude on an object of no value."

"How . . . funny of you!" said Dot.

She paused a moment, still looking at him; then with a quick, childish movement she slipped her hand through his arm. Quite suddenly she knew how to deal with him.

"You seem to forget," she said, with a little smile, "that I'm going to be your sister one day."

He stiffened at her action, and for a single moment she wondered if she could have made a mistake. And then as suddenly he relaxed. He took the hand that rested on his arm and squeezed it hard.

And Dot knew that in some fashion, by a means which she scarcely understood, she had gained a victory.

They went on together along the mossy, winding path. A fleeting shower was falling, and the patter of it sounded on the leaves.

Nap walked with his face turned up to the raindrops, sure-footed, with the gait of a panther. They were approaching the further end of the wood when abruptly he spoke.

"So you think it makes no difference?"

"Of course I do! How could it make a difference? Do you suppose—if it had been Bertie—I should have cared?"

"Bertie!" he said. "Bertie is a law-abiding citizen. And you—pardon me for saying so—are young!"

"Oh yes, I know," she admitted. "But I've got some sense all the same. And . . . and . . . Nap, may I say something straight?"

The flicker of a smile shone and died in his eyes.

"Hit as straight as you like."

"I was only going to say," she said, taking him at his word, "that if a man is a good sort and does his duty, I don't believe one person in a million cares a rap about what his parents were. I don't indeed."

She spoke with great earnestness; it was quite obvious that she meant every word. It was Dot's straightforward way to speak from her heart.

"And I'm sure Lady Carfax doesn't either," she added.

But at that Nap set his teeth.

"My child, you don't chance to know Lady Carfax as I do. Moreover, suppose the man doesn't chance to be a good sort and loathes the very word 'duty'? It brings down the house of cards rather fast, eh?"

"Oh, but you are absurd!" she exclaimed, shaking his arm with characteristic vigour. "How can you be so disgustingly flabby?"

They had reached the stile and he faced round with extended hand.

"After that—good-bye!" he said. "With your permission we'll keep this encounter to ourselves. But you certainly are a rousing evangelist. When you mount the padre's pulpit I'll come and sit under it."

Dot's fingers held fast for a moment.

"It'll be all right, will it?" she asked bluntly. "I mean . . . you'll be sensible?"

He smiled at her in a way she did not wholly understand, yet which went straight to her quick heart.

"So long, little sister!" he said. "Yes, it will be quite all right. I'll continue to cumber the ground awhile longer, if you call that being sensible. And if you think my chances of Heaven are likely to be improved by your kind intervention, p'r'aps you'll put up a prayer now and then on my behalf to the Power that casts out devils, for we are many."

"I will, Nap, I will!" she said very earnestly.

When he had gone she mounted the stile and paused with her face to the sky.

"Take care of him, please, God!" she said.

* * *

Again and yet again Anne told herself that she had been deceived, but her eyes were open at last finally and for all time. No devil's craft, however wily, however convincing, could ever close them again.

Lying in her darkened room, with her stretched nerves yet quivering at every sound, she told herself over and over that she knew Nap Errol now as a man cruel, merciless, unscrupulous, in whose dark soul no germ of love had ever stirred.

Why he had ever desired her she could not determine. Possibly her very faith in him, that faith that he had so rudely shattered, had been the attraction; possibly only her aloofness, her pride, had kindled in him the determination to conquer.

But that he had ever loved her, as she interpreted love, she now told herself was an utter impossibility.

All through the long day she lay alone with her problem, sick at heart, sick with disappointment, humiliation, and with a terrible foreboding that gave her no rest.

She had dispatched her urgent message to Lucas immediately upon her arrival at the Manor, and his prompt reply had in a measure reassured her. But she knew that he was ill, and she could not drive from her mind the dread that he might fail her.

She rose, scarcely knowing what she did, and moved across the room. Powerless, she sank upon her knees by the open window, striving painfully, piteously, vainly, to pray. But no words came to her, no prayer rose from her wrung heart. It was as though she knelt in outer darkness before a locked door.

A long, long time passed. She did not hear the rain pattering upon the green earth, nor feel the soft breeze on her neck. She had lost touch with things physical. She was yet groping in outer darkness.

A hand very softly turned the handle of her door, and a motherly face looked in.

"Why, Anne, dear child, I thought you were asleep!" the deep voice said reproachfully. "I've been listening outside for ages, and you were so quiet!"

She raised her head quickly, and in a moment rose. Her eyes were deeply shadowed, but they bore no trace of tears.

"I could not sleep," she said. "But you mustn't trouble about me. I am quite well. I will dress and come down."

Mrs. Errol came forward, shaking her head disapprovingly. "I have a note from Lucas," she said. "It arrived a quarter of an hour ago, but there was no answer, so I thought it would be real wicked to wake you up to read it."

Anne stretched out a hand that shook. "Please!" she said almost inarticulately.

With the note open in her hand she turned and sat down suddenly as if incapable of standing. The clumsy, uneven writing danced before her eyes. One sentence only, but it took her many seconds to read!

"My brother Nap leaves tonight for Arizona. *Lucas.*"

She raised her face with a deep, deep breath. She felt as if she had not breathed for hours. Silently, after a moment, she held out the brief message to Mrs. Errol.

"Thank the Lord," she said quietly.

Chapter Six

"Well, if this isn't a pleasure!" Lucas Errol said. "In fact I have something important to say to you."

"Something important!" echoed Dot. "Do tell me."

"P'r'aps I'm over-fond of regulating other folks' affairs," he said. "It's a habit that easily grows on the head of a family. But I've a sort of fancy for seeing you and Bertie married before I go out. If you tell me it's quite impossible I won't say any more."

Dot's eyes were wide.

"It would hit Bertie hard if I went under, but he wouldn't feel so badly if you were there."

"Oh, Luke," Dot broke in, her eyes full of tears. "I . . . I can't imagine this place without you."

"Say, child, I didn't mean to make you cry," Lucas exclaimed. "That was clumsy of me."

He patted her hand gently, while Dot blinked away her tears.

"Don't let us talk about it any more now," she besought him. "Oh, Lucas . . . I do want you to live, more . . . more than anything in the world, but I'll do whatever you want."

* * *

Meanwhile, Anne was thinking of Lucas, king and cripple, ruler and weakling, as she was playing at the piano. But after a while her fingers ceased to roam over the keys. She clasped them in her lap and sat still.

"My Lady!" a quiet voice said.

"Dimsdale! How you startled me!"

"I beg Your Ladyship's pardon," the old man answered.

"Are there any letters?"

"No letters, My Lady."

"Then . . ." Anne paused, and for the first time looked at the old servant attentively. "Is anything the matter?"

"Your Ladyship instructed me to open any telegram that might arrive."

"Certainly," she said. "Has there been a telegram then?"

Dimsdale's hand clenched. He looked at her anxiously.

"My Lady," he said, and stopped.

Anne sat like a statue. She felt as if her vitality were suddenly arrested, as if every pulse had ceased to beat.

"Please go on," she said, in a whisper. "There has been a telegram. Either give it to me, or . . . tell me what was in it."

He put an unsteady hand into his breast-pocket.

"It came this afternoon, My Lady, about an hour ago. I am afraid it's bad news, very bad news. I regret to say Sir Giles has been took worse, took very sudden like, and—and . . ."

"He is dead," Anne said very clearly, very steadily, in a tone that was neither of question nor of exclamation.

"He died at half past three, My Lady."

Anne took the telegram from him and moved very quietly to the window.

"Would Your Ladyship wish a message to be sent to Baronmead?"

"To Baronmead!" she said, a queer note of sharpness in her voice. "No, certainly not, most certainly not!"

And there she stopped, stopped dead as though struck dumb.

"I must write some messages at once," she said. "One of the grooms must take them. No, I shall not send for Mrs. Errol tonight. I wish to be alone . . . quite alone. Please admit no one. And . . . yes . . . tell them to pull down the blinds, and . . . shut all the windows!"

Her voice quivered and sank. She stood for a moment, collecting herself, then walked quietly to the door.

"Come to me in ten minutes for those telegrams," she said. "And after that, remember, Dimsdale, I am not to be disturbed by anyone."

And with that she passed out of the room, erect and calm, and went up to her room.

* * *

Dot and Bertie had been married very quietly and it was while they were still on their honeymoon that Capper performed the first operation on Lucas.

Anne, sitting with Mrs. Errol, waited for the verdict.

"Could you say a prayer, dear?" Mrs. Errol asked her once.

She knelt and prayed, scarcely knowing what she said, but with a passion of earnestness that left her weak.

The wind was rising. It roared in the trees and howled against the panes. Sometimes a wild gust of rain lashed the windows. It made her think of an unquiet spirit clamouring for admittance.

"Anne, dear, play to me, play to me!" besought Mrs. Errol. "If I listen to the storm I shall go mad!

No one will hear you. We are right away from his part of the house."

Although every nerve shrank at the bare suggestion, Anne rose without a single protest and went to the piano. She sat down before it, and blindly, her eyes wide, fixed, unseeing, she began to play.

What she played she knew not. Her fingers found notes, chords, melodies mechanically.

And gradually as she played there to her a curious sense of duality, of something happening that had happened before, of a record repeating itself.

She turned her head, almost expecting to hear a voice speak softly behind her, almost expecting to hear a mocking echo of the words unspoken.

"Has the Queen no further use for her jester?"

No further use! No further use! Oh, why was she tortured thus? Why, when her whole soul yearned to forget, was she thus compelled to remember the man whose brutal passion and insatiable thirst for vengeance had caught and crushed her heart?

Still she played on as one beneath a spell, while the memory of him forced the gates of her consciousness and took arrogant possession.

She saw again the swarthy face with its fierce eyes, the haughty smile, which for her was ever tinged with tenderness. Surely, oh surely, he had loved her once!

She recalled his fiery love-making and thrilled again to the eager insistence of his voice, the mastery of his touch. And then she remembered what they said of him, that women were his slaves, his playthings, the toys he broke in wantonness and carelessly tossed aside.

She remembered how once in his actual presence she had overheard words that had made her shrink, a wonder as to who was his latest conquest, the cynical remark.

"Anyone for a change and no one for long is his motto."

What was he doing now, she asked herself, and trembled. He had gone without word or message of any sort. Her last glimpse of him had been in that violent glare of lightning, inexpressibly terrible, with tigerish eyes that threatened her and snarling lips drawn back.

The vision came to her now, forcing itself upon her shrinking imagination. Vividly there rose before her his harsh face, alert, cruel, cynical, and the sinewy hands that gripped and crushed. Suddenly a shuddering sense of nausea overcame her.

She left the piano as one seeking refuge from a horror unutterable. Surely this man had never loved her . . . was incapable of love! And she had almost wished him back!

"There is someone in the entry, dear child," whispered Mrs. Errol. "Go and see . . . go and see!"

She went, moving as one stricken blind. But before she reached the door it opened and she saw Capper as through a mist of anguished fear. Then very steadily his arm encircled her, drew her tottering to a chair.

"It's all right," he said in his expressionless drawl. "The patient has regained consciousness, and, Lady Carfax, I have a message for you—the first words he spoke when he came to. He was hardly conscious when he uttered them, but I guess you'll be interested to hear what they were.

" 'Tell Anne,' he said, 'I'm going to get well.' "

The intense deliberation with which he spoke gave Anne time to collect herself.

Then Capper strolled to the window, his hands deep in his pockets. He did not turn his head till at the end of five minutes Anne came to his side. She was very pale, but quite self-possessed.

"Mrs. Errol has gone to her room," she said. "She wished to be alone."

"Gone to have a good cry, eh?" said Capper. "Healthiest thing she could do. And what about you?"

She smiled with lips that faintly quivered.

"I am quite all right, Doctor."

"You're a very remarkable woman, Lady Carfax," he said.

"I hope you may never be disappointed in me," she answered gravely.

"I hope so too," he said. "For there is a good deal dependent upon you."

"What do you mean?"

"I mean," he said. "That even I can't work miracles by myself. I can't give life. That's the woman's part. That's where I count on you. And I don't think you are going to fail me, Lady Carfax."

"I promise you I will do my utmost," she said very earnestly.

"I may be a wise man," he said, "and again I may be a meddling fool. You and the gods must decide between you. But I'm old enough to be your father anyway. So p'r'aps you'll bear with me. Lady Carfax, hasn't it struck you that a time will come, probably pretty soon, when he will begin to reach out for something that you, and you alone, can give?"

He went on in his emotionless fashion.

"He won't ask for it—anyway till he feels he can make a fair return. He will never ask a sacrifice of you. He will break his heart sooner. The point is, are you capable of offering the sacrifice unasked? For that is what it amounts to, now that the gods have cleared the way."

"Ah!" Anne said. "And . . . if . . . not?"

She spoke rather as if to gain time than because she desired an answer.

"In that case he will die, having nothing left to live for. He probably won't suffer much, simply go out like a candle. He hasn't much vitality. He may die either way. There is no responsibility attached, only possibilities."

He turned with the words, and walked across the room.

She uttered no word to stop him, nor did she move to follow. Deep in the heart of her she knew that when Lucas Errol began to reach out for something which she alone could give, it would not be in vain.

He had given of his best to her, and she was ready to give of her best in return. If she could not give him passion, she could give him that which was infinitely greater, a deep, abiding love, a devotion born of complete sympathy. She could give him happiness, and in the giving she might find it for herself.

* * *

It was nearly a month after Lucas Errol's operation that Bertie and his bride came home from their honeymoon and began the congenial task of setting their house in order.

"We must make it comfy," she said to Bertie.

He had relinquished his study of law and had resumed his secretarial duties, well aware that Lucas could ill spare him. He was in fact Lucas's right hand just then, and the burden that devolved upon him was no light one.

Lucas was very gradually gaining ground. Already he suffered less severely and slept more naturally. His last words to Capper at parting had been:

"Come again in the spring and complete the cure. I shall be ready for you."

But Bertie was not entirely satisfied.

"He doesn't say so," he told Dot, "but I believe he's bothered about Nap. Heaven knows why he should be. He was supposed to go to Arizona, but he didn't turn up there. As a matter of fact, if he never turned up again anywhere it would be about the best thing that could possibly happen."

"Oh, don't, Bertie!" Dot spoke sharply, almost involuntarily. "I don't like you to talk like that. It isn't nice of you to be glad he's gone, and . . . it's downright horrid to want him to stay away forever."

"Good heavens!" Bertie exclaimed.

"I mean it," she said, sitting up and facing him. "I don't think it's right of you, and it certainly isn't kind. He doesn't deserve to be treated as an outcast. There is a whole lot of good in him, whatever people may say. You at least ought to know him better.

"Anyhow, he is a friend of mine, and I won't hear him abused."

Bertie's face changed while she was speaking, grew stern, grew almost implacable.

"Look here," he said plainly, "if you want to know what Nap is, he's a damned blackguard, not fit for you to speak to. So, if you've no objection, we'll shunt him for good and all!"

She opened her eyes to their widest extent.

"What has he done?"

"Never mind!" said Bertie.

"But I do mind!" Swiftly indignation swamped her surprise. "Why should I shunt him, as you call it, for no reason at all? I tell you frankly, Bertie, I simply won't!"

"I have told you he is unworthy of your friendship," he said. "Let that be enough."

"That's not enough," said Dot. "I think otherwise."

"Well, if you must have it—so did Lady Carfax till she found out her mistake."

"Lady Carfax!" Dot's face changed. "What about Lady Carfax?"

"She gave him her friendship," Bertie told her grimly, "and he rewarded her with about as foul a trick as any man could conceive. You heard the story of the motor breaking down that day in the summer when he took her for a ride? It was nothing but an infernal trick.

"He wanted to get her for himself, and it wasn't his fault that he failed. It was in consequence of that that Lucas sent him away."

"Oh!" said Dot. "He was in love with her then!"

"If you call it love," said Bertie. "He is always in love with someone."

"So that was why he was so cut up," she said. "Of course . . . of course! What a mercy Sir Giles is dead! Has anyone written to tell him?"

"No," said Bertie shortly.

"But why not? Surely he has a right to know. Lady Carfax herself might wish it."

"Lady Carfax would be thankful to forget his very existence," said Bertie, with conviction.

"But surely he has a Club somewhere?"

"Yes, he belongs to the Pheonix Club, New York, if they haven't kicked him out. I'm not going to write to him. I don't want him back, heaven knows."

"Poor Nap!" said Dot gently.

That evening, when Bertie was at Baronmead, she scribbled a single sentence on a sheet of paper, thrust it into an envelope, and directed it to the Pheonix Club, New York.

"I expect it's wrong of me," she said. "But somehow I can't help feeling he ought to know."

* * *

"O God, give me rest!"

Painfully the words came through quivering lips, the first they had uttered for hours. Lucas Errol lay as he had lain for nearly three months.

At the opening of the door he did not even turn his head. Anne came to his side, her hands full of Russian violets.

"I am not disturbing you?" she asked.

She sat down beside him. Lucas was very quiet, but Anne felt he was slipping away from her.

"You are not fighting," she said accusingly.

"No." He looked at her half-wistfully from under his heavy eyelids. "Do you think me quite despicable? I've done my best."

She was silent. Perhaps she was not fully prepared to cope with his open admission of failure.

"You haven't done your best yet," Anne said, her voice very low. "You've got to hold on till the very end. It may be that help is nearer than you think."

"But if I don't want help?" he said. "It would be more merciful to let me go."

She had no answer.

"Life hasn't many inducements," he said. "I've put up a fight for it because I gave my promise to Nap before he went. But I can't win through."

"Do you think Nap would let you stop fighting?" she asked.

He smiled faintly.

"I suppose, if he were here, I should subsist on his vitality for a little while. But the end would be the same. Even he can't work miracles."

"Don't you believe in miracles?"

She paused.

"Mr. Errol," she said, "I'm going to remind you of something that I think you have forgotten. It was Dr. Capper who told me. It was when you were recovering consciousness after the operation. You sent me a message.

" 'Tell Anne,' you said, 'I am going to get well.' "

She paused for a moment, looking at him very steadily.

"I don't know why exactly you sent that special message to me, but I have carried it in my heart ever since."

She had moved him at last. She saw a faint glow spread slowly over the tired face. The heavy eyes opened wide to meet her look.

"Did I say that?" he said. "Yes, I had forgotten."

He was silent for a little, gazing full at her with the eyes of one suddenly awakened.

"Anne," he said, "do you really want me to get well? Would such a miracle make much difference to you?"

"It would make all the difference in the world," she answered earnestly. "I want it more than anything else in life."

With the words she raised her eyes, found his fixed upon her with an expression so new, so tender, that her heart stirred within her as a flower that expands in sudden sunshine, and the next moment his hand lay between her own, and all doubt, all hesitation, had fled.

"But, my dear," he said. "I always thought it was Nap. Surely it was Nap."

She felt as if something had stabbed her.

"No!" she cried passionately. "It might have been . . . once . . . before I knew him. But never since, never since!"

"Guess I must take up my burden again," he said quietly. "You won't catch me slacking any after this. And, if I don't win out, dear, you'll know that it just wasn't possible."

"Oh, but you will!" she said, clasping his hand more closely. "You will! God knows how badly I want you."

"His will be done!" said Lucas Errol. "But I want you too, dearest. I want you too."

His fingers stirred in her hold. It was the merest movement, but she knew his meaning. She slipped to her knees by his side, leaned down, and kissed him.

Chapter Seven

Christmas came and went, the most peaceful Christmas that Anne had ever known.

Lucas filled all her thoughts. Had he allowed it, she would have devoted herself exclusively to him, but this he would not have.

Very slowly, very painfully, he had struggled out of his Slough of Despond, and what that struggle had meant to him none but himself would ever know.

But, halting though it was, he did make progress. He went forward more than he slipped back. And ever he carried in his eyes the light of a great hope. She knew that he did not despair, even in his own hidden soul.

And day by day her love and admiration for the man grew and spread, filling her life, renewing her youth, transforming her very existence. No one save Mrs. Errol knew of what had passed between them. They scarcely referred to it even in private.

Entering the hall, Anne gathered up a few letters that lay there and went straight to her room. With a feeling of unwonted fatigue she dropped into an easy-chair. On her right hand she wore a ring that Lucas had given her only that day. He had half-apologised for his offering.

"If you think it premature, don't wear it!" he had said.

And she had slipped it onto her right hand and worn it ever since.

Sitting there, she raised her hand and looked closely at the gift. It was a complete circle of diamonds. She had never seen such a ring before. It must have cost a fortune. She wondered if she ought to wear it.

But suddenly memories began to crowd upon her, strive though she would.

"Do you like diamonds?" asked a casual voice.

Her hand fell into her lap. She sat as one

watching a scene upon a stage, rapt and listening. She wanted to rise and move away, to break the magic spell that bound her, to flee . . . to flee . . . but she was powerless.

"No," said the voice. "You haven't a passion for anything at present. You will have soon."

There fell a silence in her soul, a brief darkness, then again words, no longer casual, but quick, burning, passionate.

"I am mad—I am mad for you, Anne! Goddess, queen, woman, you are mine, you are mine, you are mine!"

And then, less fiery, less vehement, but infinitely more compelling:

"Where is your love for me? I will swear that you loved me once!"

The voice ceased, was lost in the wild throbbing of her heart, and Anne's hands clenched unconsciously in that moment when there came to her the conviction, inexplicable but extraordinarily vivid, that across the world Nap Errol had called to her—and had called in vain.

Minutes passed. She sat as one in a trance. Her eyes were wide and fixed. Her face was grey.

Anne Carfax did not look in her glass again that day. For the third time in her life she was afraid to meet her own eyes.

And all night long her brain thrummed like a vibrating wire to a voice that sometimes pleaded but more often gibed:

"Has the Queen no further use for her jester?"

* * *

Spring came early that year, and the day fixed for the opening of the Baronford Town Hall was brilliantly fine and warm. Anne was staying at Baronmead for the event.

The end of February was approaching. Lucas was decidedly better.

"Sweetheart," he said when she visited him. "I've had a letter from Capper."

He gave her the letter and she read that Capper expected to be in England in about a fortnight and would come down himself to ascertain if the time for the second operation had arrived.

He wrote in a cheery strain, and at the end of the letter was a postscript: "Have you taken my advice yet with regard to *la femme?"*

"An ancient joke," explained Lucas, with a smile. "He told me long ago that I should need a woman's help to pull me through. "And"—his voice dropped—"I guess he was right."

The colour came back to her face. She pressed his hand again without speaking.

"Lucas," she said, "will you take me away?"

"Yes, dear," he said.

"Far away from anywhere I have ever been before?" Her voice shook a little. "I want to begin life over again where everything is new."

* * *

Dot had asked Anne to tea when she left Baronmead. She was expecting a baby and Anne drew her on to speak of herself and her coming happiness, which she did with that sweet simplicity that had first drawn Bertie to her.

"He makes a tremendous fuss," she said. "But it's rather nice being petted for months together. I haven't had a tantrum for ages. I'm afraid I'm getting spoilt," said Dot.

"He won't be home to tea," she said when they finally turned in at the Dower House. "He stables his hunters at Baronmead, and he is sure to go in and see Luke.

"So we shall have it all to ourselves. I'm so glad, for I have been wanting your advice for days."

A glow of firelight met them from the little square hall as they entered, and a smell of cigarette smoke mingled with the scent from the burning logs.

Dot stood back for her guest to precede her, but Anne stood suddenly still.

A slim, straight figure was standing outlined against the firelight. Dot stared as she stepped forward.

"Why . . . Nap!" she said incredulously.

He made a swift elastic movement to meet her, caught her hands, laughed, and kissed her.

"Why . . . Dot!" he smiled.

And in the doorway Anne stood like a statue, the soft spring dusk behind her.

"My sister seems surprised," said Nap. "I hope I haven't come at an unlucky moment."

He did not even glance towards the silent figure in the doorway. It was as if he had not observed it.

"I am surprised," said Dot. "Hugely surprised. But I'm very glad to see you. When did you come?"

"I have been here about half an hour," he told her coolly. "I went to the Rectory first, where I learned for the first time of your marriage. You forgot to mention that detail when you wrote. Hence my brotherly salute, which you must have missed on your wedding-day!"

At this point Dot remembered her other guest, and turned with flushed cheeks.

"Anne . . . you . . . you . . . know my brother-in-law Nap?"

The pleading in her voice was unmistakable. She was suddenly agitated, wholly at a loss how to manage a most difficult situation.

But Nap hastened to relieve her of the responsibility. He had dealt with difficult situations before. He went straight to Anne and stood before her.

"Are you going to know me, Lady Carfax?" he asked.

There was no arrogance in voice or bearing as he uttered the question. He looked as if he expected to be dismissed, as if he were ready at a word to turn and go. His eyes were lowered. His foot was already on the threshold.

But Anne stood speechless and rigid. For those few seconds she was as one stricken with paralysis. She knew that if she moved or tried to speak she would faint.

She wondered desperately how long it would be before he looked up, if perhaps he would go without looking at her, or if . . . ah, he was speaking again! His words reached her as from an immense distance.

At the same instant his hands came to her out of a surging darkness that hid all things, grasping, sustaining, compelling. She yielded to them, scarcely knowing what she did.

"Lady Carfax has been overtiring herself," she heard him say. "Have you any brandy at hand?"

"Oh, dear Anne!" cried Dot in distress. "Make her sit down, Nap. Here is a cushion. Yes, I'll go and get some."

Guided by those steady hands, Anne sank into a chair, and there the constriction that bound her began to pass. She shivered from head to foot.

Nap stooped over her and chafed her icy hands. He did not look at her or speak. When Dot came back, he took the glass from her and held it very quietly to the quivering lips.

She drank, responsive to his unspoken insistence, and as she did so, for a single instant she met his eyes. They were darkly inscrutable and gave her no message of any sort. She might have been accepting help from a total stranger.

"No more, please!" she whispered, and he took the glass away.

The front door was still open. He drew it wider, and the evening air blew in across her face. Somewhere away in the darkness a thrush was warbling softly.

Nap stood against the door and waited. Dot knelt beside her, holding her hand very tightly.

"I am better," Anne said at last. "Forgive me, dear child. I suppose it has been . . . too much for me."

"My dear, dear Anne!" said Dot impulsively. "Would you like to come into the drawing-room? There is tea there. But of course we will have it here if you prefer it."

"No," Anne said. "No. We will go to the drawing-room."

She prepared to rise, and instantly Nap stepped forward. But he did not offer to touch her. He only stood ready.

When he saw that she had recovered herself so far as to be able to move with Dot's assistance, he dropped back.

"I am going, Dot," he said. "You will do better without me. I will look in again later."

And before Dot could agree or protest he had stepped out into the deepening twilight and was gone.

* * *

Mrs. Errol was smiling to herself as she drove back to Baronmead.

The car came to a stop and then as she prepared to descend she checked herself with a violent start. The man at the step who stood waiting to assist her was no servant.

"My!" she gasped. "Is it you, Nap, or your ghost?"

She walked up the steps and into the house with leaden feet. The smile had died utterly from her face. She looked suddenly old.

Abruptly she spoke, in her voice a ring of something that was almost ferocity.

"Why have you come back?"

He raised his eyebrows slightly without replying.

But Mrs. Errol was not to be so silenced. Her hands fastened with determination upon the front of his coat.

"You face me, Nap Errol," she said. "And answer me honestly. What have you come back for? Weren't there enough women on the other side to keep you amused?"

He shrugged his shoulders. "Women in plenty, amusement none. Moreover, I didn't go to be amused. Where is Lucas?"

"Don't you go to Lucas till I've talked to you."

She moved up the stairs as if she were very weary. The man behind her walked with the elasticity of a cat.

In her own room she turned and faced him.

"Nap," she said, and her deep voice quivered, "if there's any right feeling in you, if you are capable of a single speck of affection, of gratitude, you'll turn round right now and go back to the place you came from."

Nap's dark face was devoid of the faintest shadow of expression.

"That so?" he drawled. "I thought you seemed mighty pleased to see me."

She stretched out her hands to him in sudden earnest entreaty.

"Nap, tell me that it isn't Anne Carfax, and I'll bless you with my dying breath!"

"And if it were?" he said slowly, his hard eyes fixed on hers.

She choked back her agitation with the tears running down her face.

"Then God help Lucas, and me too, for it will be his death-blow!"

"Lucas?" said Nap.

He did not speak as if vitally interested, yet she answered as if compelled.

"He loves her. He can't do without her. She has been his mainstay all through the winter. He would have died without her."

"He is no better then?" he asked.

"Yes, he is better. But he has been real sick. It's only the thought of Anne that makes him able to hold on. I can see it in his eyes day after day . . . the thought of winning out and making her his wife."

"When does Capper come again?"

"Very soon now. In two or three weeks."

"If you have quite done with me, Alma Mater, I'll go."

She looked up at him apprehensively.

"What are you going to do?"

He smiled abruptly.

"I am going to get a drink."

"And what then?" she asked feverishly. "Nap, oh Nap, she is staying in the house. Won't you go, without seeing her?"

"I have seen her already," drawled Nap.

"You have seen her?"

His smile became contemptuous.

"What of it? Do you seriously suppose she is the only woman in the world I care to look at?"

"I don't know what to think," cried Mrs. Errol. "I only know that you hold Luke's fate between your hands."

He was already at the door. He turned and briefly bowed.

"You flatter me, Alma Mater!"

With the smile still upon his lips he left her.

"Boney, old chap, you're the very man I want!"

Such was Lucas Errol's greeting to the man who had shot like a thunderbolt into the peaceful atmosphere that surrounded him, to the general disturbance of all others who dwelt therein.

"I guess you must have known it," he said, the sinewy hand fast gripped in his. "You've come like an answer to prayer. Where have you been all the time? And why didn't you write? It's worried me not hearing."

Nap sat down, leaving his hand in his brother's grasp. The cynicism had gone utterly from his face, but he did not answer either question.

"So you are winning out?" he said. "It's been a long trail, I'll wager."

"Oh, damnably long, Boney." Lucas uttered a weary sigh. "I was nearly down and out in the winter. But I'm better, you know. I'm better. What's the verdict?"

"I'll tell you presently. You're not looking

overfed anyway." Nap's fingers began to feel along his wrist. "Did Capper say he wanted a skeleton to work on?"

"Shucks, dear fellow! There's more than enough of me. Tell me about yourself. What have you been doing? I want to know."

"I?" Nap jerked back his head. "I've nothing to tell. You know what I want to do. Well, I've done it, and that's all there is to it."

He laughed, stretched his arms above his head, and made a vehement gesture as if flinging something from him, something that writhed and clung.

"Will it interest you to know that the devil has ceased to provide me with distractions?" he asked suddenly.

A certain eagerness came into the blue eyes. "That so, Boney?"

Nap leaned back and stared at the ceiling. "It's no virtue of mine," he said. "I found I wanted solitude, so I went to the Rockies and stayed there till I was tired. That's all."

"Old chap, I'm real glad," the tired voice drawled. "You've found yourself at last. I always felt you would—sooner or later."

Nap's lips twitched a little. "Don't be too sure of that. Anyway, it doesn't follow that I shall sit at home and practise the domestic virtues. I've got to wander a bit first and find my own level."

"Not yet, dear fellow. I'm wanting you myself."

"You!" The thin lips began to smile. "That's

real magnanimous of you. But, thanks all the same. I guess I'm not essential."

"And I guess you can do more for me than anyone else," Lucas made quiet reply. "P'r'aps you'll think me a selfish brute to say so, but I need you badly. You're like a stimulating drug to me. You pick me up when I'm down. There is no one can help me in the same way."

"You wouldn't get Capper to say 'Amen' to that," remarked Nap.

"Capper is no oracle out of his own sphere. Besides," there was almost a note of pleading in Lucas's voice, "I know what I want better than he can tell me."

"True, very true!" Nap was smiling somewhat grimly. "And doubtless your wish is law. But it doesn't follow that you always desire what is best for yourself. Hadn't you better consult the Queen before you admit the wasp to the hive?"

Lucas was watching him gravely, his brows still drawn. "Boney," he said slowly at length. "I'd give a good deal to see into your soul."

Nap smiled with a faint return of cynicism.

"Afraid I can't show you what I haven't got."

Lucas passed the rejoinder by. "What makes you conclude that I am more to her than—any other man?"

"Circumstances," said Nap.

"What circumstances?"

"Finding her installed here as one of the family, for one. Finding you pulling off the biggest deal of your life, for another. And other signs, crowds of them, that I can't explain but that I can't fail to notice when I've got my nose to the trail. You needn't be shy about it. I'm just as pleased as you are."

But Lucas's face did not clear. There followed a very decided pause. Then, with an effort, very earnestly, he spoke.

"Nap, I don't believe you'll lie to me when I tell you that I'd rather die than be deceived. I know you cared for her once."

"I care for most women," said Nap indifferently. "What of that? It's the way I'm made, and I must say they don't most of 'em seem to mind."

"But, Boney—Anne Carfax?"

Nap threw up his head with a brief laugh.

"Oh, I'm cured of that, quite cured. The paths of perpetual virtue are not for me. I prefer more rapid travelling and a surer goal."

He stood up, his arms stretched up above his head.

"I make you a present of Anne Carfax," he said lightly. "Not that she is mine to give. But I wouldn't keep her if she were. We belong to different spheres."

"And yet . . ." Lucas said.

"My dear fellow, that's an old story." Impulsively Nap cut in, almost fiercely. "Do you think the woman is living who could hold me after all this time? I tell you that fire is burnt out. Why rake over the dead ashes?"

"I am looking for the Divine Spark," Lucas answered quietly.

"And if you found it?" Nap's words came through smiling lips, and yet they sounded savage.

"If I found it," very steadily came the answer, "I would blow it to a flame, Boney, for your sake, and hers."

"For hers?" Something fierce showed in Nap's eyes. It was as if a goaded animal suddenly looked out of them.

Lucas must have seen it, for on the instant his manner changed.

"We won't go any further," he said. "Only, dear fellow, I can't part with you yet. Let that be understood. I want you."

"Sobeit!" said Nap. "I will stay and see you married."

And with the words he stooped and grasped his brother's hand for a moment.

"Go on and prosper, Luke," he said. "It's high time that you came into your own."

* * *

As soon as Anne entered Baronmead that evening she was aware of a difference. Bertie, with a thunderous countenance, came forward to meet her. She had not seen him wear that look in all the months of Nap's absence.

"The prodigal has returned," he told her briefly. "P'r'aps you know."

She did not pretend to misunderstand him.

She had schooled herself to face the situation without shrinking.

"Yes, I know," she said. "I met him at your house an hour ago."

"At my house!"

"He didn't stay," she said rather wearily. "What of Luke? Has he seen him?"

"Can't understand Luke," muttered Bertie. "He's actually pleased. Say, Lady Carfax, would it help any if I were to stop and dine?"

"No," Anne said, smiling a little. "Go back to Dot. She is expecting you."

Nap did not present himself at the dinner-table, and Ann dined alone with Mrs. Errol, and she went to Lucas as usual when the meal was over, but she thought he seemed tired and she did not remain with him long.

He kept her hand for a moment when she stooped to bid him good-night.

"Anne," he said gently. "I just want you to know, dear, that Nap will be all right. Don't be anxious. There is no need."

He desired to reassure her, she saw; and she bent and kissed him. And then for a moment a queer gust of passion possessed her, shook her from head to foot.

"Oh, Luke," she whispered, "can't you send him away again?"

He looked up at her oddly, with eyes that seemed to see beyond her.

"Good-night, dear," he said, as if he had not heard.

She turned from him in silence. It was the first time she had ever appealed to Lucas Errol in vain.

She went to her room early that night. She told herself she must leave on the morrow. She was urged by a deep unrest. She could not remain under the same roof with this man who had once so cruelly tortured her. She could not. Lucas must understand this. He must never ask it of her, never . . . never!

And yet in the morning she went down with a calm aspect, resolute and unafraid. Once more she was compelling herself to do simply that which lay nearest to her hand.

Nap came out of a room near the foot of the stairs as she descended. He scarcely looked at her, but quite obviously he had been awaiting her coming.

"May I have two words with you before you join the mater?" he asked.

With her whole soul she wanted to refuse. Yet without visible hesitation she yielded. She turned aside into the room he had just quit.

He followed, and, closing the door, came forward to the table. Anne waited for a moment or two.

"What is it you wish to say to me?" she asked at length.

At the first sound of her voice he ceased to work, but still he did not raise his eyes.

"On my own account, nothing," he said, speaking very deliberately. "But as my sojourn here may be an offence to you, I think it advisable to explain at the outset that I am not a free agent. My brother has decreed it, and as you know his word is my law."

"I understand," said Anne gravely, but even as she spoke she was asking herself what possible motive had prompted this explanation.

He jerked up his head and she caught the glint of his fiery eyes for an instant.

"You—care for Lucas, Lady Carfax?" he said.

Her heart gave a sudden throb that hurt her intolerably. For a moment she could not speak.

"Yes," she said. "I love him."

Nap was pulling mechanically at the rag he held. It began to tear between his hands. She watched him ripping it to shreds. Suddenly he seemed to realise what he was doing, and tossed it from him. He looked her straight in the eyes.

"Have you fixed the date for your coronation?" he asked.

Her eyes fell instantly.

"Will you tell me what you mean?" she said.

"Is my meaning obscure?"

She compelled herself to answer him steadily. "If you mean our marriage, it will not take place for some time, possibly not this year."

"Why not?" said Nap. "Are you a slave to etiquette?"

The thing seemed preposterous on his lips. She faintly smiled.

"The decision does not lie with me."

"Ah!" he said shrewdly. "The privilege of

Kings! You will still be a Queen before you are thirty. And your first act will be to expel the Court jester, if he waits to be expelled."

She saw his grim smile for an instant, and knew that he was playing his old fencing game with her, but at the same time she knew that there was no antagonism behind his point.

How the knowledge came to her she could not have said, but she realised afterwards that it was at that moment that she began to perceive that the devil had gone out of Nap Errol.

The conviction was slow in growing, but it was then that it first took root; it was then that her fear of the man began to die away.

She raised her eyes.

"Why should I do that, Nap?"

He made her a deep bow.

"Because I have been unfortunate enough to incur your displeasure."

There was a moment of silence; then, in obedience to that instinct to which in rare moments she yielded herself and which never played her false, Anne held out her hand to him.

"I forgive you," she said.

He started. He evidently had not expected that from her. Perhaps he had not wanted it. Later she wondered. But he showed no awkwardness of indecision. Only once had she ever seen him at a loss, and of that once she would never voluntarily think again.

He took her hand upon his sleeve and bent over it. She thought he was going to kiss it, and a sharp dread went through her. But he only touched it for a single instant with his forehead.

"For Luke's sake?" he said, not looking at her.

"For your own," she made answer, almost as if she could not help herself.

"Because . . . ?" he questioned.

"Because I know you love him," she said. "Because I know that you will be loyal to him."

"Though I may be false to you?" he said.

"I am only a woman. I am afraid your experience of women has not taught you to respect them."

"My experience of one woman at least," he said, "has taught me . . . something different, something I am not likely to forget."

It was the end of the interview. In silence Anne turned to go. He wheeled round and opened the door for her, but he did not look at her again nor she at him.

When the door closed between them she felt as if a great silence had fallen in her life.

* * *

On the day succeeding Nap's return, Dot went to tea at Baronmead. She was a very constant visitor there. Lucas always enjoyed her bright presence and welcomed her with warmth. But Dot was not feeling very bright that day. She looked preoccupied, almost worried.

"Come right in," said Lucas hospitably. "It's good of you to come and see me like this."

She took his outstretched hand, looking at

him anxiously. She saw that he had not slept for many hours. Though he smiled at her, there was a grey look about his lips that made her wonder if he was in pain.

"Sit down," he said gently. "It's nothing. Only another bad night. I can't expect to sleep soundly always."

"How disappointing!" Dot murmured.

"Not surprising though. I had an exciting day yesterday. You heard of Nap's return?"

"Yes. I saw him."

"Well?" said Lucas.

She turned to him impulsively.

"Isn't it horrid when the thing you've been planning for and wanting ever so long happens and everyone else is cross?"

The blue eyes looked quizzical.

"Very, I should say," said Lucas. "Would it be presumptuous to ask what has been happening and who is cross?"

Dot's answering smile held more pathos than mirth. Her lips took a quivering, downward droop.

"It's Nap," she said.

He raised his brows a little.

"Nap seems the general pivot on which all grievances turn," he remarked.

"I do so hate making mistakes," she said.

"We all do it," said Lucas.

"Oh, you don't!" She turned and gravely regarded him. "You are always wise," she said, "never headlong."

"Which only demonstrates your ignorance and the kindness of your heart," said Lucas. "But go on, won't you? What has Nap been doing?"

"Oh, nothing. Nap is all right. It isn't Nap I mind. It . . . it's Bertie," whispered Dot. "I . . . I . . . it's very ridiculous, isn't it? I'm a wee bit afraid of Bertie, do you know?"

"St. Christopher!" said Lucas, in astonishment.

"Yes. But you won't ever tell him, will you?" she pleaded anxiously. "If . . . if he knew or guessed . . . all my prestige would be gone. I shouldn't be able to manage him at all. He . . . he is rather difficult to manage sometimes, don't you think?"

Lucas was frowning slightly.

"I guess I can manage him," he said.

"No doubt you could. I expect you always have. He respects you," said Dot, with unwitting wistfulness.

Lucas turned his head and looked at her very steadily.

"Will you tell me something, Dot?" he said.

She nodded.

"Why are you afraid of Bertie?"

She hesitated.

"Come!" he said. "Surely you're not afraid of me too!"

"No," she said tremulously. "I'm not such a little idiot as that, Luke. I'm afraid of Bertie because . . . because I've done something he wouldn't like. It's a very little thing, Luke. It is really. But . . . but it's bothered me off and on all the winter. And now that Nap is home, I feel much worse . . . as if

. . . as if it had been really wrong. And . . . and I know I ought to tell him. But . . . I can't."

"Tell me," said Lucas gently.

"And you will tell him for me?"

"If you wish me to do so."

"I don't like it," sobbed Dot. "It's so despicable of me. I've wanted to tell him for ever so long. But he has been so good to me all this time, and . . . and somehow I couldn't face it.

"We haven't even squabbled for months now. It . . . it seemed such a pity to spoil everything when it really didn't make any difference to anyone if he knew or not."

"Don't cry," interposed Lucas. "It would hurt Bertie if he knew."

"Dear Bertie!" whispered Dot. "Isn't it horrid of me to be such a coward? I haven't done anything really wrong, either. In fact at the time it seemed almost right."

"Almost!" said Lucas, faintly smiling.

She smiled also through her tears.

"Why don't you call me a humbug? Well, listen! It was like this. One night in the beginning of the winter Bertie and I had a disagreement about Nap. It wasn't at all important.

"But I had to stick up for him, because I had chanced to see him just before he left in the summer . . . you remember. When he was very, very miserable."

"I remember," said Lucas.

"And I was frightfully sorry for him," Dot went on, "though at the time I didn't know what was the matter. And I couldn't let Bertie say horrid things about him. So I fired up.

"And then Bertie told me"—she faltered a little—"about . . . about Nap caring for Lady Carfax. And that was where the trouble began. He didn't give him credit for really loving her, whereas I knew he did."

"That so?" said Lucas.

"Oh, I was sure," she said. "I was sure. There are some things a woman can't help knowing. It was the key to what I knew before. I understood . . . at once."

"And then?" said Lucas.

"Then, of course, I remembered that Lady Carfax was free. And I asked Bertie if he knew. You see, I thought it possible that in her heart she might be caring for him too. I knew they had always been friends.

"And it seemed only fair that Nap should know that Sir Giles was dead. I told Bertie so. He didn't agree with me." Dot paused and vigourously dried her eyes before she continued.

"It seemed to me a matter of fair play. He didn't know where Nap was, only his Club address. And he wouldn't write himself, so I just wrote a single line telling Nap that Sir Giles was dead, and sent it off that night.

"Now that has brought him back, and Bertie is so angry with him for returning. And Anne nearly fainted when she saw him. I felt as if I had landed everybody in a hopeless muddle."

"Don't fret," said Lucas very kindly. "I wanted him."

"You think as I do? You think he cares for Anne?"

"I guess so," he answered, "since your letter brought him back."

"And . . . and Anne? Do you think . . . do you really think . . . ?"

"I guess so," he said again.

He lay silent for a while, his eyes drooping heavily, till she began to wonder if he was falling asleep.

"Dot," he said, "have I your permission to make what use I like of this?"

She gave a slight start.

"You are going to tell Bertie?"

"My dear, I think Bertie had better know."

"I know he ought. But he will be furious with me."

"Not if I talk to him," said Lucas, with his quiet smile.

"But it's so mean of me," she protested. "And I'm sure it's bad for you."

He reached out his hand to her.

"No, it isn't bad for me, Dot. It's just the best thing possible. You've put me in the way of something great."

"Do you really think you can make things go right?"

"Under God," said Lucas gravely.

* * *

Notwithstanding Lucas's assurance, Dot awaited her husband's coming in undisguised trepidation that night.

She was convinced that Bertie was going to be very angry with her, and her heart sank the more she thought of it.

The door opened and she heard Bertie's voice.

"The car will be all right," he said. "It's a fine night. Go in, won't you? I expect Dot is waiting."

And with amazement Dot saw Nap enter the hall in front of her husband.

He came straight to her just as he had come on the previous day, and she had a moment of sheer panic lest he should have the effrontery to kiss her; but he spared her this, though the smile with which he greeted her told her that he was quite aware of her embarrassment and its cause.

"Bertie has taken upon himself to ask me to dine," he said, as he held her hand. "I hope that is quite agreeable?"

"Of course I am delighted," she said, but her eyes sought Bertie's somewhat anxiously.

She saw with relief that the cloud had gone from his face. He came forward, bent, and kissed her. His hand lay upon her shoulder for an instant with a quick, reassuring touch, and she knew that all was well.

"Heavens, child! How cold you are!" he said. "I'll bring you down a shawl, shall I? Come along, Nap. We are late."

During dinner Nap was plainly upon his best behaviour. He seemed determined that Bertie should be on easy terms with him, and he was in a great measure successful. Though reticent, Bertie was undoubtedly cordial.

At the appearance of the dessert, Nap rose.

"I must be getting back to Lucas," he said.

"Oh, skittles! He won't be wanting you," Bertie protested. "Sit down again, man. You haven't been here an hour."

"No, I must go," Nap answered.

"It isn't going to be a walk over to make Lucas well, but I guess we'll pull it off between us."

"Amen!" said Bertie fervently.

And Nap wrung his hand and departed. For the first time in their lives there was a friendly understanding between them.

For the first time Bertie was aware of a human heart throbbing behind that impenetrable mask.

Chapter Eight

It was growing late that night when Lucas opened his eyes after a prolonged and fruitless attempt to sleep, and found Nap standing at the foot of the bed watching him.

"Hullo, dear fellow! I never heard you come in."

Nap stepped noiselessly to his side.

"Don't talk!" he said. "Sleep!"

"I can't sleep. It's no use. I was only pretending." Lucas stifled a sigh of weariness.

Nap stooped over him and laid steady hands upon his wrists. His hold was close and vital; it pressed upon the pulses as if to give them new life.

"You can sleep if you try," he said.

Lucas shook his head with a smile.

"I'm not a good subject, Boney. Thanks all the same!"

"Try!" Nap said insistently.

But the blue eyes remained wide.

"No, old chap. It's too high a price to pay, even for sleep."

"What do you mean?"

"I mean that I'm afraid of you, Boney."

"Skittles!" said Nap.

"Yes, it may seem so to you; but you see, I know what you are trying to do."

"What am I trying to do?" demanded Nap.

Lucas paused for a moment; he was looking straight up into the harsh face above his own.

"I know you," he said. "I know that you'll get the whip hand of me if you can, and you'll clap blinkers on me and drive me according to your own judgment. I never had much faith in your judgment, Boney. And it is not my intention to be driven by you."

There was no resentment in the tired voice, only unflagging determination.

"You don't trust me then?"

"It's your methods I don't trust, dear fellow, not your motives. I'd trust them to perdition."

"But not my—honour?" Nap's lips twisted twisted over the word.

Lucas hesitated.

"I believe you would be faithful to your own code," he said at length.

"But you don't consider that to trick a man who trusted me would be against that code?"

On the instant Lucas spoke, in his voice was a tremor that was almost passionate.

"Boney, Boney, old chap, have I wronged you? God knows I've tried to be just. But are you straight? Are you honest? I'd give my soul to be able to trust you. Only, dear fellow, forgive me, I can't!"

Nap's hands clenched. "Why not?" he said.

"Because," very slowly and painfully Lucas made reply, "I know that you are trying to blind me. I know that you are sacrificing yourself, and another, in order to deceive me.

"You are doing it to save me pain, but—before God, Boney—you are torturing me in the doing far more than you realise. I'd sooner die ten times over than endure it. I can bear most things, but not this—not this!"

Silence followed the words, a silence that was vital with many emotions. Nap stood upright against the lamplight. He scarcely seemed to breathe, and yet in his very stillness there was almost a tinge of violence.

"It's no manner of use your trying to deceive me any longer," Lucas went on. "I happen to know what brought you back, and I'm thankful to know it. After all, her happiness comes first with both of us, I guess. That's why I was so almighty pleased to see you in the first place. That's why it won't hurt me any to let her go to you."

Nap made a sharp movement and came out of his silence.

"Luke, you're mad!"

"No, Boney, no! I'm saner than you are. When a fellow spends his life as I do, he has time to look all round things. He can't help knowing. And I'm not a skunk. It never was my intention to stand between her and happiness."

"Happiness!" Harshly Nap echoed the word. "Don't you know that she only tolerates me for your sake? She wouldn't stay within a hundred miles of me if it weren't for you."

"Oh, shucks, Boney!" A faint smile touched the worn face on the pillow. "I know you hurt her infernally. But she would forgive you that, women do, you know, though I guess she would have forgiven you easier if she hadn't loved you."

"Man, you're wrong!" Fiercely Nap flung the words. "I tell you there is no love between us. I killed her love long ago. And as for myself . . ."

"Love doesn't die," broke in Lucas Errol quielty. "I know all about it, Boney. Guess I've always known. And if you tell me that your love for Anne Carfax is dead, I tell you that you lie!"

With a sudden fierce movement Nap dropped

down upon his knees beside the bed, flinging his arms wide over his brother's body in such an agony of despair as Lucas had never before witnessed.

"I wish I were dead!" he cried out passionately. "I wish to heaven I had never lived!"

It was a cry wrung from the very depths of the soul, a revelation of suffering of which Lucas had scarcely believed him capable. It opened his eyes to much that before he had but vaguely suspected.

He laid a hand instantly and very tenderly upon the bowed head.

"Shucks, Boney," he remonstrated gently. "Just when you are wanted most!"

A great sob shook Nap.

"Who wants me? I'm nothing but a blot on the face of creation, an outrage, an abomination, a curse!"

"You're just the biggest thing in that woman's life, dear fellow," answered the tired voice. "You hang on to that. It'll hold you up, as God always meant it should."

Nap made an inarticulate sound of dissent, but the quiet restraint of his brother's touch seemed to help him. He became still under it, as if some spell were upon him.

"Did you think I'd cut you out, Boney? Mighty lot you seem to know of me! It's true that for a time I thought myself necessary to her. Maybe, for a time, I was. She hadn't much to live for anyway.

"But I never imagined that I ruled supreme.

I know too well that what a woman has given once she can never give again. I didn't expect it of her. I never asked it. She gave me what she could, and I, I did the same for her.

"But that bargain wouldn't satisfy either of us now. No, no! We'll play the game like men, like brothers. And you must do your part. Believe me, Boney, I desire nothing so earnestly as her happiness, and if when I come to die I have helped to make this one woman happy, then I shall not have lived in vain."

Nap turned his head sharply.

"Don't talk of dying! You couldn't die! And do you seriously imagine for a single instant that I could ever give her happiness?"

"I imagine so, dear fellow, since she loves you."

"I tell you she wouldn't have me if I asked her."

"You don't know. Anyway, she must have the chance; if she doesn't take it, well, she isn't the woman I imagine her to be."

"She's a saint," Nap said with vehemence. "And you, Luke, you're another. You were made for each other. She would be ten million times happier with you. Why do you want her to marry a blackguard?"

"You are not a blackguard, Boney. I always said so. And the love of a good woman will be your salvation. You're wrong. I couldn't give her real happiness. There is only one man in the world can give her that. And I—am not that man."

He paused.

"Say, Nap, I believe I could sleep now," he said.

"Yes, yes, old chap, you shall." Nap raised himself abruptly. "Guess you won't be afraid now that you have got your own way. But just one thing more. You'll be wanting all your strength for yourself for the next few weeks. Will you, for my sake if you like, put all this by till you are winning out on the other side? She would say the same, if she knew."

"I trust you, Boney, absolutely, implicitly, from the bottom of my soul."

The words left Lucas Errol's lips with something of the solemnity of an oath. He held out a quiet hand.

"Now let me sleep," he said.

Nap rose. He stood for a moment in silence.

"Good-night, dear chap!" he said in a whisper, and with the words he stooped and kissed the lined forehead of the man who trusted him. . . .

Half an hour later the door of the adjoining room opened noiselessly and Tawny Hudson peered in.

One brother was sleeping, the quiet, refreshing sleep of a mind at rest. The other sat watching by his side with fixed inscrutable eyes.

The latter did not stir, though in some indefinable way he made Tawny Hudson know that he was aware of his presence, and did not desire his closer proximity.

Obedient to the unspoken command, the

man did not come beyond the threshold; but he stood there for many seconds, glowering with the eyes of a monstrous, malignant baboon.

* * *

The second time that Tawny Hudson was driven from his master's side was on a day of splendid spring—English April at its best.

Till the very last moment he lingered, and it was Lucas himself with his final, "Go, Tawny!" who sent him from the room. They would not even let him wait, as Nap was waiting, till the anaesthetic had done its work.

Black hatred gripped the man's heart as he crept away. What was Nap anyway that he should be thus honoured? The cloud that had attended his coming had made a deep impression upon Hudson.

He had watched the lines upon his master's face till he knew them by heart. He knew when anxiety kept the weary eyes from closing.

He knew when the effort of the mind was more than the body could endure. Of Lucas's pleasure at his brother's return he raised no question, but that it would have been infinitely better for him had Nap remained away he was firmly convinced.

And he knew, with the sure intuition which unceasing vigilance had developed in him, that Capper thought the same.

Capper resented as he did the intrusion of the black sheep of the family. But Capper was obviously powerless when it came to removing Nap.

There was a mysterious force about Nap that no one seemed able to resist. He, Hudson, had felt it a hundred times, had bowed to it in spite of himself. He called it black magic in his own dark heart, and because of it his hatred almost amounted to a mania.

It was nearly one o'clock when at last the closed door opened. Bertie was on his feet in an instant. Dr. Randal came quietly out, glanced round, and stopped.

"It is over. We have taken him into the inner room, and he is recovering consciousness. No, don't go to him. His man mustn't go either. We want all these doors open, wide open, the windows too. But no one is to go near. He must have absolute quiet."

Bertie decided to remain for the night, and at a late hour he saw Capper for a moment. The great man's face was drawn and haggard.

"He won't last through the night," he said. "Tell the ladies to be in readiness. I will send for them if there is time."

"No hope whatever?" said Bertie.

Capper shook his head. "I fear—none. He is just running down—sinking. I think you had better not come in, but stay within call."

Inside the room, it was nearly an hour after midnight when a voice spoke in the utter silence.

"Boney!"

"I'm here, old chap."

"Good-bye, dear fellow!" It was scarcely more than a whisper. It seemed to come from closed lips.

"Open your eyes," said Nap.

Slowly the heavy lids opened. The blue eyes

met the deep, mysterious gaze focussed upon them.

"Ah, but, Boney . . ." the tired voice said, as though in protest.

And Nap's voice, thrilled through and through with a tenderness that was more than human, made answer.

"Just a little longer, dear old man! Only a little longer! See! I'm holding you up. Turn up the lamp, Doctor. Take off the shade. He can't see me. There, old chap! Look at me now. Grip hold of me. You can't go yet. I'm with you. I'm holding you back."

Capper trickled something out of a spoon between the pale lips, and for a little there was silence.

But the blue eyes remained wide, fixed upon those other fiery eyes that held them by some mysterious magic from falling into sightlessness.

Three figures had come in through the open door, moving wraith-like, silently. The room seemed full of shadows.

After a while Lucas spoke again, and this time his lips moved perceptibly.

"It's such a long way back, Boney, no end of a trail, and all uphill."

"Don't be faint-hearted, old chap! I'll haul you up. It won't be so tough presently. You're through the worst already. Hold on, Luke, hold on!"

Again Capper poured something between the parted lips, and a quiver ran through the powerless body.

"Hold on!" Nap repeated. "You promised you

would. You mustn't go yet, old boy. You can't be spared. I shall go to the devil without you."

"Not you, Boney!" Lucas's lips quivered into a smile. "That's all over. You're playing—the straight game—now."

"You must stay and see it through," said Nap. "I can't win out without you."

"Ah!" A long sigh came pantingly with the word. "That so, Boney? Guess I'm—a selfish brute —always was—always was."

Anne, standing apart, was cut to the heart with the pathos of it. But Nap did not seem to feel it. He knelt on, inflexible, determined, all his iron will, all his fiery vitality, concentrated upon holding a man in life.

In the morning the fight was over. In the morning Lucas Errol had turned, reluctantly as it seemed to Anne, from the Gate of Death.

* * *

For three weeks after the operation Capper said nothing good or bad of his patient's condition, and during those weeks he scarcely went beyond the terrace. He moved about like a man absorbed, and it seemed to Anne whenever they met that he looked at her without seeing her.

Nap was even closer in his attendance, and Tawny Hudson found himself more than ever supplanted and ignored. For night and day Nap was at hand, sleeping when and how he could, always alert at the briefest notice, always ready with unfailing nerve and steady hand.

And Capper suffered him without the smallest remonstrance. He seemed to take it for granted that Nap's powers were illimitable.

"That young man will kill himself," Dr. Randal said once. "He is living at perpetual high pressure."

"Leave him alone," growled Capper. "He is the force that drives the engine. The wheels won't go round without him."

And this seemed true; for the wheels went round very, very slowly in those days. Lucas Errol came back to life, urged by a vitality not his own, and the Shadow of Death still lingered in his eyes.

On the day that Capper and Nap set him on his feet for the first time, his weakness was such that he fainted; but he recovered and apologised, and would even have faced the ordeal again had Capper permitted it.

On the following day he went through it without a tremor, and slept thereafter for hours, scarcely rousing himself for nourishment.

It was during that sleep that Nap left him, went out into the spring woods, and remained absent for some time. Lucas was still sleeping when he returned and after a brief look at him he moved away into the adjoining room and prowled to and fro there, waiting.

At the first sound of his brother's voice he was back by the bedside. Lucas smiled a welcome.

"I'm better," he said, and held up a weak hand.

It was the first time he had made the assertion. Nap took the hand and laid it gently down.

"You'll get well now," he said.

"I don't know where I'd be without you, Boney," he said. "Do you know you're looking awfully ill?"

"Shucks!" said Nap.

"You'll go to bed in your own room tonight," said Lucas, "go to bed and sleep."

In the morning he knew with sure intuition that Lucas would summon him. Almost he knew what he would say.

The call came at last, very quiet and deliberate.

"Boney! Come here a minute, old chap. No, I'm not wanting anything, only a word in private. Say, Boney, is Anne still stopping here?"

He had seen her nearly every day since the operation, but he had been too drowsy to ask any questions. He had only smiled upon her, and sometimes for a little had held her hand.

"She is backwards and forwards," said Nap. "I believe she is spending tonight."

"Ah! Then, Boney, I want you to speak to her—tonight."

He looked up at his brother with his old, kindly smile.

"It's for my own sake, old chap," he said. "You know, I didn't sleep last night. I was thinking about her—about you both. And I want her to know everything tonight. I shall sleep the easier when she knows."

Nap stood silent. His face was set in hard lines.

"Will you tell her, Boney?"

"What am I to tell her?" said Nap.

"Tell her the truth, dear fellow, so that she understands it. Make her realise that the dearest wish of my life is her happiness—and yours. Remember, I came back because of it. It will be my happiness too."

"She won't have me, you know," Nap said, after a moment. "She only forgave me because of you."

"Shucks, dear fellow! I guess that wasn't the reason."

"I wish to heaven you'd let me off," Nap said with sudden vehemence. "Let me shunt first instead of last. It's more than I can face, even for you."

"But I guess you'll face it all the same," said Lucas gently. "And when it's over, come, both of you, and tell me."

He closed his eyes and turned his face to the sunshine.

"So long, old chap!" he said. "Don't stay indoors. I'm not wanting you. Think I'll get to sleep presently. Don't let them wake me if I do."

But Nap lingered, still holding his hand. "Luke!" he said.

There was a note of entreaty in his voice, but, for the second time in his life, Lucas turned a deaf ear. The smile was still on his lips, but his eyes remained closed.

"Go, dear fellow!" he said softly. "And God bless you!"

And Nap turned with a set face and went straight from the room.

* * *

It was drawing towards evening on that same day when Anne, who had been spending the afternoon at the Dower House, walked back across the park.

She went by way of the stream along which she and Nap had once skated hand in hand in the moonlight, and as she went she stooped now and then to gather the flowers that grew in the grass beside her path. But her face as she did it was grave and thoughtful. She did not seem to notice their fragrance.

As she neared the lake she moved more slowly, and reaching a rustic seat beneath a cedar that shadowed the entrance to the gardens she sat down, her grey eyes fixed upon the water that gurgled at her feet.

And in that moment she knew that she was not alone. How she knew it she could not have said. No sound or shadow told her. No hand touched her. Yet she knew.

For a few seconds she stood motionless on the edge of the stream. Then without turning she spoke.

"Were you looking for me?"

"Yes," he said.

He came to her side. They were close, close to that spot where once he had so arrogantly claimed her friendship. Today it seemed she had no word to utter.

For a space she waited; then, finding in his silence something that disquieted her, she spoke again.

"Is all well? Why are you not with Lucas?"

"All's well," he said, but he left her second question unanswered. He was gazing down intently into the clear water.

Her heart began to throb with thick, uneven strokes. What had he come to say to her? And why did he stand thus silent? There was something tragic about him, something almost terrible.

She waited beside him in wordless foreboding. Whatever was coming she felt powerless to avert. She could only brace herself to meet the inevitable.

In some fashion, though he never glanced her way, he must have been aware of her agitation, for when he spoke again there was some measure of reassurance in his voice, emotionless though it was.

"I shan't alarm you," he said. "I shan't even ask you to answer me, much less to treat me kindly. But you've got to hear me, that's all."

He paused.

"I'm not telling you for my own sake, only because Luke has ordained that you must know. I daresay you thought it strange that I should have come back so soon. It probably made you wonder."

"It did," said Anne, in a low voice.

"I knew it would. I am here to explain. I knew the odds were dead against me when I started, as they are today.

"All the same, you are to understand that I came back when I did because I had just heard that you were free, and I was mad enough to dream that in spite of everything I should one day persuade you to marry me."

Anne still waited beside him, her hands clasped tightly upon her drooping flowers.

He continued very rapidly, as if he wished to have done.

"That was my true reason for coming back. I don't know if I deceived you any on that point. I tried to. But anyway I didn't manage to deceive Lucas. He sees most things. He knows for instance that I care for you."

Almost angrily he flung the words.

"And he thinks you ought to know it, in case you care for me. It's a preposterous idea anyway. But he won't be easy till I've given you the chance to trample on me. He thinks I owe you that. Maybe I do. Well, you have your opportunity."

"Do you think I want . . . that?" Anne said, her voice very low.

"I can't say," he replied. "Most women would. But, if you want to know, I'd sooner be trampled. I've promised I'll play the straight game, and I'm playing it. I'm telling you the raw truth. I love you. I have it in me to make you know it. But . . ."

"But you love Lucas better."

He nodded.

"Just that. Also, Lucas is a good man. He will set your happiness first all his life. While I, while

I," he said, speaking very quietly, "might possibly succeed in making you happy, but it wouldn't be the same thing.

"You would have to live my life, not I yours. I am not like Lucas. I shouldn't be satisfied with—a little."

"And you think that is all I can offer him?" she said.

"I have no theories on that subject. I believe you would satisfy him. I believe, ultimately, you would both find the happiness we are all hunting for."

"And you?" Anne said, her voice very low.

He straightened himself with a backwards fling of the shoulders, but still he did not look at her.

"I don't fit into the scheme of things anyway," he said grimly. "I was just pitchforked into your life by an accident. It's for you to toss me out again."

Anne was silent. She stood with her face to the sinking sun. She seemed to be gathering her strength.

"What will you do?" she asked in the same hushed voice. "Where will you go?"

He turned slowly towards her.

"I really don't know. I haven't begun to think."

His eyes looked deeply into hers, but they held no passion, no emotion of any sort. They made her think with a sudden intolerable stab of pain of that night when he had put out the fire of his passion to receive her kiss.

He had told her once that that kiss was the greatest thing that had ever happened to him. Did he remember it now? she wondered, as she met those brooding eyes, still and dark and lonely as they had been then, unfathomable as a mountain pool.

A vast, surging pity filled her soul. She understood him so well . . . so well.

"Nap," she said tremulously, "what can I say to you? What can I do?"

He put out a quiet, unfaltering hand and took hers.

"Don't be too good to me," he said. "Don't worry any on my account. If you do, maybe Luke will notice and misunderstand. He's so damnably shrewd."

A brief smile crossed his face.

"I'll tell you what to do, and when it's done you'll feel better. Come with me now to Lucas, it's his own idea, and tell him you've no use for me. Put it how you like. Women can always do these things.

"Make him know that he comes first with you still and always will. Tell him you know all the truth and it hasn't made you change your mind. Tell him you'd rather belong to a man you can trust. He'll believe you, Anne. We all do."

He spoke insistently. He had begun to draw her towards the path. But as they reached it, his hand fell from hers. He walked beside her, close beside her, but not by word or touch did he seek further to persuade her.

So side by side in silence they went back to the house.

"He may be asleep," Nap said. "Shall I go first?"

She assented without speaking. Somehow the spell of silence seemed to hold her also.

"Follow me in a minute," he said. "if I don't come back."

And with that he glided through the narrow space and passed from sight. A minute later, Anne softly pushed back the door and entered. . . .

Nap was crouched motionless with outflung arms across the foot of the bed, and she saw that Lucas Errol was lying asleep with his face to the sky, and the lines of pain were smoothed utterly away.

On his lips was a smile which some call the Stamp of Death, others call the shining reflection of the Resurrection Glory the passing soul has left behind.

* * *

Those to whom Lucas was dearest shed the fewest tears. Standing in the hallowed stillness beside her dead son, Mrs. Errol turned to Anne, saying softly, "The Lord knows best, dear. We wouldn't call him back. He wouldn't want to come."

Up to the last minute Anne was doubtful as to whether Nap would attend his brother's funeral. She walked with Capper immediately behind Bertie and his mother. Neither of them seemed to expect Nap, or even to think of him.

His movements were always sudden and generally unaccountable. But she knew that his absence would cause comment in the neighbourhood, and though she also knew that Nap would care nothing for that, she earnestly hoped that he would not give occasion for it.

Nevertheless, the procession started without him, and she had almost ceased to hope when he suddenly appeared from nowhere, as it seemed to her, and walked on her other side.

When all was over, Nap disappeared, and she saw no more of him till the evening, when for the first time he came to the dinner-table. Capper was leaving early on the following day, and it was to this fact that Anne attributed Nap's appearance.

Bertie dined at home, but he walked over later to take leave of Capper.

"I wish you would tell me what to do with Tawny Hudson," he said. "I believe the fellow's crazy; and he's pining too. I don't believe he has eaten anything for days."

Since Lucas's death Tawny Hudson had attached himself to Bertie, following him to and fro like a lost dog, somewhat to Dot's dismay; for, deeply though she pitied the great half-breed, there was something about him that frightened her.

"I don't know what to do with him," Bertie said. "He's as gaunt as a wolf. He's hanging about somewhere outside now. Wish you'd take him along to America with you, Doctor."

"Call him in," said Capper, "and let me have a look at him."

Bertie went to the door.

"Hudson!" he called. "Tawny! Where are you?"

But there came no answer out of the shadows. The only voice which Tawny would obey was still.

Bertie came back baffled.

"Confound the fellow! I know he's within hail."

"Leave the brute alone!" said Nap. "He isn't worth much anyway."

"But I can't let him die," said Bertie.

"I'll take him back with me if you're wanting to be rid of him," said Capper. "Tell him so if you get the chance."

"Thanks!" said Bertie. "But I don't believe he'll budge. Nap will be crossing next week. P'r'aps I shall persuade him to go then."

He looked across at Nap.

"I know you don't like the fellow, but it wouldn't be for long."

"Probably not," said Nap, staring fixedly at the end of his cigar.

Something in his tone made Anne glance at him, but as usual his face told her nothing. She saw only that his eyes were drawn as if with long watching, and that the cynical lines about his mouth were more grimly pronounced than she had ever seen them before.

Not long after, Bertie got up to go. His farewell to Capper was spoken almost in a whisper, and Anne saw that his self-control was precarious.

When he shook hands with her he was beyond speech.

She was glad to see Nap rise and accompany him, with a friendly hand pushed through his arm.

For nearly half an hour longer she sat on with Capper; then at length she rose to go.

"I shall see you in the morning," she said, pausing.

"I am making an early start," said Capper.

"I shall see you all the same. Good-night."

She went to the door and stood there for several seconds. The voice of a nightingale thrilled through the silence. Was it only a year . . . only a year . . . since the veil had been rent from her eyes?

Slowly her tears passed. There came again to her that curious sense as of something drawing her, almost as of a voice that called. The garden lay still and mysterious in the moonlight.

She caught its gleam upon a corner of the lake where it shone like a wedge of silver.

For a few seconds she stood irresolute; then without word or backward glance she stepped down into the magic silence.

Her feet carried her noiselessly over the grass to that shining splendour of water, and turned along the path that led past the seat under the cedar where Nap had joined her on that evening that seemed already far away, and had told her that he loved her still.

By this path he and Bertie would have gone

to the Dower House; by this path he would probably return alone.

Her heart quickened a little as she passed into the deep shadow. She was not nervous as a rule, but there was something mysterious about the place, something vaguely disquieting. The gurgle of the stream that fed the lake sounded curiously remote.

She turned towards the rustic seat on which she had rested that day, and on the instant her pulses leapt to sudden alarm.

There was a stealthy movement in front of her; a crouching object that looked monstrous in the gloom detached itself from the shadow and began to move away.

For a moment she thought it was some animal; then there came to her the unmistakable though muffled tread of human feet, and swift as an arrow comprehension pierced her.

The thing in front of her was Tawny Hudson.

But why was he skulking there? Why did he seek thus to avoid her? What was the man doing? The agitated questions raced through her brain at lightning speed, and after them came a horrible, sickening suspicion.

Whence it arose she could not have said, but the memory of Nap's face only half an hour before, when Tawny Hudson had been under discussion, arose in her mind and confirmed it almost before she knew that it was there.

She had often suspected the half-breed of harbouring a dislike for Nap. And if he were really crazy, as Bertie believed, to what lengths might he not carry it?

Fear stabbed her, fear that was anguish. At any moment now Nap might be returning, and if Tawny were indeed lying in wait for him . . .

She traversed the deep shadow cast by the cedar and looked forth into the park beyond. The man had disappeared. He must have doubled back among the trees of the shrubbery.

Was he hoping that she would turn and go back by the way she had come, leaving him free to accomplish his purpose, whatever it might be?

Then her heart suddenly stood still, for away in the distance, walking with his light, swinging gait over the moonlit sward, she saw Nap.

In that moment her fear took definite and tangible form, and a horror of the thing that lurked in the shadows behind her seized her, goading her to action. She passed out into the quiet moonlight and moved to meet him.

Nap did not see her at once. The background of trees obscured her. But as she drew away from them he caught sight of her, and instantly quickened his pace.

They met scarcely fifty yards from the cedar, and breathlessly Anne spoke.

"Turn back with me a little way. I have something to say to you."

They walked several paces before Anne spoke again.

"You will think me very strange, but I have had a fright. I . . . I want you, Nap, to . . . to understand and not think me foolish or laugh at me."

"I couldn't do either if I tried," said Nap. "Who has been frightening you? Tawny Hudson?"

"Yes." Anne was still breathless; she glanced nervously over her shoulder. "Shall we walk a little faster? He . . . he is lurking in those trees, and do you know I don't think he is safe? I think . . . I can't help thinking . . . that he is lying in wait for you to . . . to do you a mischief."

Nap stopped dead.

"That so? Then I reckon I will go and deal with him at once."

"Oh no!" She gasped. "No! Nap, are you mad?"

He gave her a queer look.

"By no means, though I believe I should be if I went any further with you. You stay here while I go and investigate."

He would have left her with the words, but on the instant desperation seized Anne. Her strained nerves would not bear this. She caught his arm, holding him fast.

"You must not! You shall not! Or if you do, I am coming with you. You . . . you are not going alone."

"I am going alone," Nap said; but he stood still, facing her, watching her as he had watched her on that day long ago when he had lain helples in her arms in the snow, the day that revelation had first come to her shrinking heart.

"I am going alone," he repeated very deliberately. "And you will wait here till I come back."

She felt that he was putting forth his strength to compel her, and he was stronger than she.

She did not understand his ascendancy over her, but she could not help being aware of it.

"Oh, don't go!" she entreated weakly. "Please don't go! I can't bear it. It . . . it's too much. Nap, if . . . if any harm comes to you, I . . . I think it will kill me."

There came a sudden gleam in his sombre eyes that seemed to stab her, but it was gone instantly, before he spoke in answer.

"You are not foolish, you are sublime. But, be wise as well." Very quietly he extricated his arm from her clinging hands and turned to go. "Don't watch. Go on to the bridge and wait for me there."

He was gone. Blindly she obeyed him. She reached the bridge and leaned upon the hand-rail. She strained her ears to listen, but she could hear naught else; and for a time she actually lacked the physical strength to turn and look.

At last, after the passage of many minutes, she summoned her sinking courage. Faint and dizzy still, she managed to raise her head. The moonlight danced in her eyes, but with immense effort she compelled herself to look back.

The next instant utter amazement seized and possessed her, dominating her fear. Nap was standing, a straight, relentless figure, while at his feet grovelled and whimpered the great half-breed Tawny Hudson.

The next instant Nap turned upon his heel and came towards her, while Tawny Hudson got up and slunk away into the shadows.

Anne awaited him, standing quite motionless. She knew now what had happened. He had grappled with the man's will just as once he had grappled with hers. And he had conquered.

She expected him to approach her with the royal swagger of victory, and involuntarily she shrank, dreading to encounter him in that mood, painfully aware of her own weakness.

He came to her.

"Anne, forgive me!"

She gazed at him in astonishment.

"Forgive you!" she repeated. "But why?"

"I have no right to practise the black arts in your presence," he said, "though as a matter of fact there was no other way. I've frightened the poor devil out of his senses. Aren't you frightened too?"

"I don't understand," she answered rather piteously. "I am only thankful that you are not hurt."

"That's good of you," he said, and she heard no irony in his voice.

He leaned his arms upon the rail beside her, and stared down in silence for several moments into the dark water.

"If this had happened a week—less than a week—ago," he said at length, speaking very quietly, "I would have let the fellow knife me with the utmost pleasure. I should even have been grateful to him. And you would have had cause for gratitude, too, for Luke would have been with you today."

She shrank a little at his words.

"I don't understand," she said again.

He stood up and faced her with abrupt resolution.

"I am going to make you understand," he said, "once and for all. It's a rather hideous recital, but you had better hear it. I will condense it as much as possible. I've been an evil brute all my life, but I guess you know that already.

"The first time I saw you I wanted to ruin you. I never meant to fall in love with you. I kicked against it—kicked hard. Good women always exasperated me. But I wanted a new sensation, and, by heaven, I got it!"

He paused a moment, and she saw his grim features relax very slightly.

"I was caught in my own net," he said. "I believe there is magic in you. You captured me, anyway. I did homage to you, in spite of myself. After that night the relish went out of everything for me. I wanted only you."

Again he paused, but she said nothing.

"But you kept me at a distance," he said, "and I couldn't help myself. That was the maddening part of it. Lucas knew even then, or suspected. But he didn't interfere. He saw that you were taming me. And so you were. But that thrashing upset everything.

"It drove me mad. I was crazy for revenge.

Lucas made me go away, but I couldn't stay. I was like a man possessed. My hatred for your husband had swamped my love for you. You have got to know it, Anne; I am like that.

"I wanted to wreak my vengeance on him through you, because I knew, by then, that I had somehow reached your heart.

"And so I came to you, I saw you, and then I couldn't do it. Your love—I suppose I may call it that?—barred the way. It was your safeguard. You trusted me, and for that I wanted to fall down and worship you.

"But you sent me away, and I had to go. You made a man of me. I lived a clean life because of you. I was your slave. I believe I should have remained so if your husband had died then. But the knowledge that he was coming back to you was too much for me. I couldn't stand that. I broke free."

He stopped suddenly.

"I needn't go into what happened then," he said. "You saw me at my worst, and—you conquered me. You drove me out of your stronghold, and you locked the door. I don't know even now how you did it. None but a good woman would have dared.

"Do you know, when I came to my senses and knew what I had done, knew that I'd insulted you, killed your trust, your love, made you despise me, I nearly shot myself.

"It was Dot who kept me from that. She

guessed, I suppose. And I went away—I went right away into the Rockies, and fought my devils there. I came back saner than you have ever known me, to hear that you were free.

"Can you believe that I actually told myself that you were mine, mine for the winning? I stretched out my hands to you across half the world, and I felt as if wherever you were I had somehow managed to reach and touch you. It was exactly a year from the day I had first met you."

"Ah! I remember!" Anne said, her voice quick with pain; but she did not tell him what she remembered.

He went on rapidly, as if she had not spoken.

"And then I came to you. And—I found—I found Luke—in possession. Well, that was the end of everything for me. I couldn't help knowing that it was the best thing that could possibly happen to either of you. And I—well, I was just out of it.

"I would have gone again that night, but Luke wouldn't have it. He wouldn't let me drop out, but neither would I let him. I fought every inch. I wouldn't let him die. I held him night and day, night and day.

"I knew what it meant to you too. My whole soul was in it, but even so, I couldn't hold on forever. I had to slacken at last, and he—he slackened too. I knew it directly, felt him losing hold. That was two days before he died.

"I pulled myself together and grabbed him again. I think he knew. He tried to wake up, said he'd get well, made me let go of him, made me explain things to you. And then—well, I guess he thought his part was done—so he just—let go."

Abruptly he turned from her and leaned again upon the rail.

"That's all," he said. "But if Tawny had taken it into his fool brain to make an end of me a little sooner—as I meant him to—I know very well Luke would have hung on—somehow—for your sake. Oh, I wish to heaven he had.

"I'm not fit to speak to you, not fit to touch your hand. You—you—I believe you'd be kind to me if I would let you. But I won't—I won't! I'm going away. It rests with me now to protect you somehow, and there is no other way."

He ceased to speak, and in the silence she watched his bent head, greatly wondering, deeply pitying.

"You see how it is with me, Anne," he said very sadly. "Tawny Hudson thinks I'm a devil, and I'm not sure, even now, that he isn't right. That's why I'm going away.

"I won't have you trust me, for I can't trust myself. And you have no one to protect you from me. So you won't blame me for going? You'll understand?"

His words went straight to her heart. She felt the quick tears rising, but she kept them back. She knew that he needed strength from her just then.

After a moment she answered him.

"I think you are quite right to go, Nap. And

. . . yes, I understand. Only . . . someday . . . someday . . . come back again!"

He leaned towards her. His face had flushed into sudden vitality at her words. He made a movement as if he would take her into his arms.

Then abruptly he withdrew himself, and gripped his hands together behind him. Standing, with the moonlight shining on his face, he showed her that which her heart ached to see.

For though the dusky eyes were fixed and still, unveiled but unrevealing, though the high cheekbones and lantern jaw were grim as beaten brass, she had a glimpse of the seething, volcanic fires she dreaded, and she knew that he had spoken the truth. It was better for them both that he should go.

"I will come back to you, Anne," he said, speaking very steadily. "I will come back to you, if I find I can."

It was final and she knew it. She held out her hand to him in silence, and he pressed it dumbly against his lips.

Chapter Nine

"Isn't he just dear?" Mrs. Errol asked.

There was a cooing note in her deep voice. She sat in the Dower House garden with her grandson upon her knees.

"Isn't he sweet, Anne?" she said.

"He's a lord of creation," she said. "And he knows it already."

"Where is Bertie?" Dot asked. "He had to go to town, but he promised to be back early for his son's first birthday-party. It's such an important occasion!"

She rose and slipped a hand through Anne's arm.

"Let's go and look for him. I know he can't be long now. The son of the house likes having his granny to himself. He never cries with her."

They moved away together through the sunlit garden.

"Anne darling, I've got something to tell you, something you very possibly won't quite like," Dot said suddenly.

"What is it, dear?" asked Anne.

The smile had gone from her face, but her eyes were steadfast and very still.

"My dear," said Dot, "it's only that Bertie didn't go up to town on business. It was to meet someone, and . . . that someone will be with him when he comes back. I promised Bertie to tell you, but you were so late getting here I was afraid I shouldn't have time. Oh, Anne dear, I do hope you don't mind."

"It is all right," Anne said, and with the words she smiled again, though her face was pale. "It is quite all right, Dot dear. Don't be anxious."

"That's the motor coming. Oh, Anne, I've only told you just in time!"

A moment more and the car whizzed into the drive. There came a yell of welcome from Bertie at the wheel and the instant checking of the motor.

And the man beside Bertie leaned swiftly forward, bareheaded, and looked straight into Anne's white face.

She did not know how she met his look. It seemed to pierce her. But she was nerved for the ordeal, and she moved towards him with outstretched hands.

His fingers closed upon it as he stepped from the car, gripped and closely held it. But he spoke not a word to her; only to Dot.

"I seem to have stumbled into a family gathering," he said when they gave him the place of honour between Mrs. Errol and his hostess.

"Being one of the family, I guess it's a happy accident," said Mrs. Errol.

He bowed to her elaborately.

"Many thanks, Alma Mater! Considering the short time you have had for preparing a pretty speech of welcome, it does you undoubted credit."

"Oh, my, Nap!" she said. "I'm past making pretty speeches at my age. I just say what I mean."

A gleam of surprise crossed his dark face.

"That's so, Alma Mater?" he said. "Then, considering all things, again thanks!"

He turned from her to the baby sprawling on a rug at his feet, and lifted the youngster to his knee.

"So this is the pride of the Errols now."

The baby stared up at him with serious eyes, and very deliberately and intently Nap stared back.

"What is his name, Dot?" he asked at length.

"Lucas Napoleon," she said.

"Good heavens!" he ejaculated. "What an unholy combination! What in thunder possessed you to call him that?"

"Oh, it wasn't my doing," Dot hastened to explain, with her usual honesty, "though of course I was delighted with the idea. Bertie and I called him Lucas almost before he was born."

"Then who in wonder chose my name for him?" demanded Nap.

"My dear Nap, what does it matter?" broke in Dot.

"Let me take him," Anne said.

She stooped to lift the boy, who held out his arms to her with a crow of pleasure. Nap looked up at her, and for an instant only their eyes met; but an understanding dawned upon Nap's face.

Dot declared afterwards that the birthday-party had been all she could have desired. Everyone had been nice to everyone, and the baby hadn't been rude to his uncle, a calamity she had greatly feared.

Also, Nap had improved, hugely improved. Didn't Bertie think so? He seemed to have got so much more human. She couldn't realise that there had ever been a time when she had actually disliked him.

"P'r'aps we're more human ourselves," suggested Bertie; a notion which hadn't occurred to Dot, but which she admitted might have something in it.

Anyway, she was sure Nap had improved, and she longed to know if Anne thought so too.

Anne's thoughts upon that subject, however,

were known to none, perhaps not even to herself. All she knew was an overwhelming desire for solitude.

She scarcely slept at all that night, yet when she rose, some of the bloom of youth had come back to her, some of its summer splendour was shining in her eyes.

"Dimsdale," she said, "Mr. Errol is coming over this morning. I expect him to luncheon."

"Mr. Errol, My Lady?"

"Mr. Nap Errol. Show him into the garden when he comes. He is sure to find me somewhere."

When breakfast was over Anne sat with closed eyes, seeming to hear the very heart of creation throbbing in every sound, yet listening, listening intently, for something more.

It was a very little thing at last that told her her turn had come, so small a thing, and yet it sent the blood tingling through every vein, racing and pulsing with headlong impetus like a locked stream suddenly set free.

It was no more than the flight of a startled bird from the tree above her.

She opened her eyes, quivering from head to foot. Yesterday she had commanded herself. She had gone to him with outstretched hands and welcoming smile. Today she sat quite still. She could not move.

He came to her, stooped over her, then knelt beside her. The sunlight streamed down upon his upturned face. His eyes were deep and still and passionless.

"You expected me," he said.

She looked down at him.

"I have been expecting you for a very long time."

A flicker that was scarcely a smile crossed his face.

"And yet I've come too soon."

"Why do you say that?"

"Because, my Queen," he said, "the *role* of jester at Court is obsolete, at least so far as I am concerned, and I haven't managed to qualify for another."

"Do you want another?" she said.

He turned his eyes away from her.

"I want—many things," he said.

She motioned him to the seat beside her.

"Tell me what you have been doing all this time."

"I can't."

But he rose and sat beside her as she desired.

"What under heaven have I been doing?" he said. "I don't know. I guess I've been something like Nebuchadnezzar when they turned him out to grass. I've just been—ruminating."

"Is that all?"

There was a curious note of relief in Anne's voice.

His old magnetic smile flashed across his face as he caught it.

"That's all, Queen Anne. It's been monstrous dull. Do you know, I don't think Heaven intended me for a hermit."

Involuntarily almost, she smiled in answer. Her heart was beating quite steadily again. She was no longer afraid.

"Nebuchadnezzar came to his own again," she observed.

"He did," said Nap.

"And you?"

He leaned back with his face to the sky.

"Not yet," he said.

Anne was silent. He turned after a moment and looked at her.

"And what have you been doing, O Queen?"

Her hands were clasped in her lap. They suddenly gripped each other very fast.

"Won't you tell me?" said Nap.

He spoke very softly, but he made no movement towards her. He sat aloof and still. Yet he plainly desired an answer.

It came at last, spoken almost in a whisper.

"I have been . . . waiting."

"Waiting . . ." he said.

She parted her hands suddenly, with a gesture that was passionate, and rose.

"Yes, waiting," she said. "Waiting, Nap, waiting! And oh, I'm so tired of it. I'm not like you. I have never wanted . . . many things; only one . . . only one!"

Her voice broke. She turned sharply from him. Nap had sprung to his feet. He stood close to her. But he held himself in check. He kept all emotion out of his face and voice.

"Do you think I don't know?" he said. "My

dear Anne, I have always known. That's the damnable part of it. You've wanted truth instead of treachery, honour instead of shame, love instead of . . ."

"Don't say it, Nap!"

He took her hand, drew it to his heart, and held it there.

"And you say you don't want many things," he went on, in a tone half-sad, half-whimsical. "My dear, if I could give you one tenth of what you want you'd be a lucky woman and I a thrice lucky man. But we've got to face it—I can't.

"I thought I could train myself, fashion myself, into something worthy of your acceptance. I can't. I thought I could win back your trust, your friendship, last of all your love. But I can't even begin. You can send me away from you if you will, and I'll go for good and all.

"On the other hand, you can keep me, you can marry me."

He paused; and she fancied that she felt his heart quicken.

"You can marry me," he said again, "but you can't tame me. You'll find me an infernal trial to live with. I'm not a devil any longer. No, and I'm not a brute. But I am still a savage at heart, and there are some parts of me that won't tame."

He drew in his breath.

"My love for you is a seething furnace, an intolerable craving. I can't contemplate you sanely. I want you unspeakably."

His hold had tightened. She could feel his heart

throbbing now like a fierce thing caged. His eyes had begun to glow. The furnace door was opening. She could feel the heat rushing out, enveloping her. Soon it would begin to scorch her.

Yet she knew no shrinking. Rather, she drew nearer, as a shivering creature starved and frozen draws near to the hunter's fire.

He went on speaking rapidly, with rising passion.

"My love for you is the one part of me that I haven't got under control, and it's such a mighty big part that the rest is hardly worthy of mention. It's great enough to make everything else contemptible. I've no use for lesser things. I want just you, only you, for the rest of my life!"

He stopped suddenly, seemed on the verge of something further, then pulled himself together with a sharp gesture.

"I'm afraid that's all there is to me," he said. "Lucas would have given you understanding, friendship, chivalry, all that a good woman wants. I can only offer you—bondage."

At the end of several breathless moments she spoke, and in her voice was a deep note that thrilled like music.

"There is a bondage," she said, "that is sweeter than any freedom. And, Nap, it is the one thing in this world that I want . . . that I need . . . that I pray for night and day."

"Anne!" he exclaimed.

He turned back to her.

"Anne," he said again, speaking rapidly, in a

voice that shook. "I have tried to play a straight game with you. I have warned you. I am not the right sort. You know what I am. You know."

"Yes," Anne said, "I know." She raised her head and looked him straight in the eyes. "You are all the world to me, Nap. You are the man I love."

His arms caught her, crushed her fiercely to him, held her fast.

"Say it again!" he said, his fiery eyes flaming. "Say it! Say it!"

But Anne did not speak. Only for a long, long second she gazed into his face; then in utter silence she turned her lips to his.

* * *

They spent the whole of the long June day together in the garden. Neither knew how the time went till evening came upon them all unawares, a golden evening of many fragrances.

They came at last along the green path under the lilac trees, and by the rustic seat Nap stopped.

"I'll leave you here," he said.

She looked at him in surprise.

"Won't you dine with me?"

"No," he said restlessly. "I won't come in. I should stifle under a roof tonight."

"But we will dine outside," she said.

He shook his head.

"No, I'm going, Anne." He caught her hand to his lips. "I hate leaving you. How long must I be condemned to it?"

She touched his shoulder with her cheek.

"Don't you know that I hate it too?"

"Then . . ."

"Next week, Nap."

"You mean it?"

"Yes. I mean it."

"You will marry me next week. What day?"

"Any day," she said, with her face against his shoulder.

"Any day, Anne? You mean that? You mean me to choose?"

She laughed softly.

"I shall leave everything to you."

"Then I choose Sunday," Nap said, without an instant's consideration. "As early in the morning as possible. I shall go straight to the Rector and arrange it right now."

"Very well," she said. "I'll try to be ready."

He threw up his head with the old arrogant gesture.

"You must be ready," he said imperiously. "I shall come and fetch you myself."

She laughed again at that. "Indeed you will not. I shall go with Mrs. Errol."

He conceded this point, albeit grudgingly.

"And afterwards?" he said.

"The afterwards shall be yours, my darling."

"You mean that?"

"Of course I mean it."

"Then, Anne"—he bent his face suddenly, and his lips moved against her forehead—"will you come with me to Bramhurst?"

"Bramhurst!"

She started. The name was a bitter memory

among the many other bitter memories of her life.

"Will you?"

"If you wish it," she answered gently.

"I do wish it."

"Then . . . so be it."

He bent his head a little lower, kissed her twice passionately upon the lips, held her as if he could not bear to let her go, then tore himself almost violently from her, and went away, swift and noiseless as a shadow over the grass.

* * *

It was late on the evening of her wedding-day that Anne entered once more the drawing-room of the little Inn at Bramhurst and stopped by the open window.

She stood looking out. It was a night of wonder, of marvellous soul-stilling peace. Yet her brows were slightly drawn as she waited there. She seemed to be puzzling over something.

"Say it out loud."

She did not start at the words though Nap had come up behind her without sound. She stretched out her hand without turning, and drew his arm through hers.

"Why did we choose this place?"

"You didn't choose it."

"Then you?"

"I chose it chiefly because I knew you hated it," he said, a queer vibration of recklessness in his voice.

"Am I to believe that?"

He looked at her through the falling dusk, and his hand closed tense and vital upon her arm.

"It's the truth anyway," he said. "I knew you hated the place, that you only came to it for my sake. And I made you come because I wanted you to love it."

"For your sake, Nap?" she said softly.

"Yes, and for another reason."

He paused a moment; speech seemed suddenly an effort to him.

"You forgave me, I know, long ago; but I want you here, on this spot, to tell me that what happened here is to you as if it had never been. I want it blotted out of your mind forever. I want your trust, your whole trust!"

It was like a hunger-cry rising from the man's very soul. At sound of it she turned impulsively.

"Nap, never speak of this again! My dearest dear, we need not have come here for that. Yet I am glad now that we came. It will be holy ground to me as long as I live, and I shall remember that it was here that the door of paradise was opened to us at last, and that God meant us to enter in."

She lifted her eyes to his with a look half-shy, half-confident.

"You believe in God," she said.

He did not answer at once. He was looking out beyond her for the first time, and the restless fire had gone out of his eyes. They were still and deep as a mountain pool.

"Nap," she said in a whisper.

Instantly his look came back to her. He took her face between his hands with a tenderness so new that it moved her inexplicably to tears.

"I believe in the Power that casts out devils," he said very gravely. "Luke taught me that much. I guess my wife will teach me the rest."

ABOUT THE EDITOR

BARBARA CARTLAND, the celebrated romantic author, historian, playwright, lecturer, political speaker and television personality, has now written over 150 books. Miss Cartland has had a number of historical books published and several biographical ones, including that of her brother, Major Ronald Cartland, who was the first Member of Parliament to be killed in the War. This book had a Foreword by Sir Winston Churchill.

In private life, Barbara Cartland, who is a Dame of the Order of St. John of Jerusalem, has fought for better conditions and salaries for Midwives and nurses. As President of the Royal College of Midwives (Hertfordshire Branch), she has been invested with the first Badge of Office ever given in Great Britain, which was subscribed to by the Midwives themselves. She has also championed the cause for old people and founded the first Romany Gypsy Camp in the world.

Barbara Cartland is deeply interested in Vitamin Therapy and is President of the British National Association for Health.